*The House
of a Thousand Floors*

OTHER TITLES IN THE SERIES

Prague Tales
Jan Neruda

Skylark
Dezső Kosztolányi

Be Faithful Unto Death
Zsigmond Móricz

The Doll
Boleslav Prus

The Adventures of Sindbad
Gyula Krúdy

The Sorrowful Eyes of Hannah Karajich
Ivan Olbracht

The Birch Grove and Other Stories
Jaroslaw Iwaszkiewicz

The Coming Spring
Stefan Żeromski

The Poet and the Idiot and Other Stories
Friedebert Tuglas

The Slave Girl and Other Stories on Women
Ivo Andrić

Martin Kačur—The Biography of an Idealist
Ivan Cankar

Whitehorn's Windmill or, The Unusual Events Once upon a Time in the Land of Paudruvė
Kazys Boruta

The Tower and Other Stories
Jānis Ezeriņš

A Tale of Two Worlds
Vjenceslav Novak

Three Chestnut Horses
Margita Figuli

The Prose of the Mountains. Three Tales of the Caucasus
Aleksandre Qazbegi

The House of a Thousand Floors

Jan Weiss

Translated from the Czech by Alexandra Büchler

Central European University Press
Budapest • New York

English translation copyright © 2016 Alexandra Büchler

Published in 2016 by

Central European University Press
An imprint of the
Central European University Limited Liability Company
Nádor utca 11, H-1051 Budapest, Hungary
Tel: +36-1-327-3138 or 327-3000
Fax: +36-1-327-3183
E-mail: ceupress@pree.ceu.edu
Website: www.ceupress.com

224 West 57th Street, New York NY 10019, USA
Tel: +1-732-763-8816
E-mail: meszarosa@press.ceu.edu

All rights reserved. No part of this publication may be reproduced, stored in a retrieval system, or transmitted, in any form or by any means, without the permission of the Publisher.

ISBN 978-963-386-070-0
ISSN 1418-0162

Originally published as *Dům o tisíci patrech* in 1929 by Melantrich.
The translation of this volume is based on the 1964 edition by Naše vojsko.

Copy-editing: Linda Jayne Turner and Robin Wright

The translation of this volume has been supported by the Ministry of Culture of the Czech Republic.

Library of Congress Cataloging-in-Publication Data

Names: Weiss, Jan. | Büchler, Alexandra, translator.
Title: The house of a thousand floors / Jan Weiss ; translated from the Czech by Alexandra Büchler.
Other titles: Dům o tisíci patrech. English
Description: New York : Central European University Press, 2015. | Series: CEU Press classics
Identifiers: LCCN 2015036178| ISBN 9789633860700 (pbk.) | ISBN 9789633860717
(pdf)
Classification: LCC PG5038.W45 D813 2015 | DDC 891.8/635—dc23
LC record available at http://lccn.loc.gov/2015036178

Printed in Hungary by Prime Rate Kft.

Contents

Translator's Note   VII

The House of a Thousand Floors   1

Afterword   261

Translator's note

When I was growing up in Czechoslovakia, *Dům o tisíci patrech* was one of my favourite books. This remained so long after I emigrated, and I often wondered why it had never been translated into English, since this literary gem had made its way into many other European languages, including French, German, Greek, Italian, Polish, Portuguese and Russian. When I was asked to choose a title to translate for CEUP's modern classics series, I seized the opportunity to give readers around the world access to this major work of modern Czech literature in English.

Translating *Dům o tisíci patrech*, I was faced with the task of rendering Weiss's highly dramatic, expressionistic style into English, a language which does not easily accommodate stylistic exultation with multiple exclamation marks and dashes. At the risk of being seen as a translator using excessive domestication, I decided to remove a great many of these punctuation marks to make the English translation flow more smoothly.

Translator's note

Switching from the past tense to the present and back again is another characteristic feature of Weiss's style, as is fluctuation between first and third person singular. Both are devices which aim to heighten the dramatic impact of the narrative but could result in some confusion and make following the sequence of tenses in English virtually impossible. Here again, my editors and I agreed that we had to use these stylistic devices sparingly for the sake of clarity and adherence to English grammatical structures.

Characters' names presented another dilemma and, in this case, the decision was to keep the names of various characters and places throughout, without domesticating them in any way; the name of the protagonist Petr Brok (Peter Bullet, Pellet or Shot in English) retains its Czech form, as do the various German, French, Hungarian, Italian, Spanish and Russian personal names, appellations and titles which give the novel its distinctly cosmopolitan flavour.

When it comes to the word central to the entire work, the name of the nightmarish "house of a thousand floors" which in the original is alternately called Mullerdóm – echoing the word for cathedral and the pan-Slavic word for house – and Mullerton, suggesting a phantasmagorical vertical "city", we opted for Mullerdom throughout. The suffix means domain, jurisdiction or realm in English rather than house, thus playing with the ending of the word "kingdom", but at the same time nods towards the original use of the word.

Alexandra Büchler

I

*It started with a dream · A man on the staircase
· The red carpet · Who am I?*

It was a terrible dream. A hollow skull filled with darkness and, within the centre, a flickering yellow light. Below, a game of cards is being played, but the cold is such that colours disappear beneath a layer of frost. And then a wide platform, as if suspended in the air – with a row of people lying on it, all lined up on their left sides, warming each other with stiffening knees and frozen laps. If one moves, the entire chain of bodies is set in motion, the S-shaped links become unstuck, the chain is broken as the bodies turn onto the other side. And there they become glued together again, knees bending, laps interlocking. – But no-one is warmed any more. They slowly turn cold, pierced by a long icy skewer...

Suddenly, a gigantic hand seizes the skull with its infernal vision and hurls it into flames. – The skull cracks open! A terrible, unbearable pain – and then – awakening!

A man woke up from a heavy dream. His gaze followed the sloping ceiling. His first thought was:

Where am I?

Jan Weiss

A staircase! The first step, covered with a red carpet, had served as a cushion for his dream. A scarlet hanging rope formed the railing, and, on the other side, a diagonal row of ascending marble cones.

Where am I?

The man sprang up. Up or down?

Up!

Taking the steps two or three at a time. A deserted landing between two floors, with no windows and no doors. And again the red-carpeted staircase. Another floor, blind and deaf, with a white lamp hanging from the ceiling. Red carpet. Up. – The scarlet rope, like an endless snake on his right, and those ascending cones on the left.

When was this going to end? Where were the doors? The man keeps running up. His head is spinning and the scarlet cascade of the staircase is burning into his brain.

Suddenly he stops. Perhaps... perhaps it would be better to run down instead, to go back. No, it's too late. I've come up too far now. Have to keep going.

Another floor! – And another! Can't go on!... One last floor! And another, equally desolate, with its tongue of red carpet hanging out.

His heart cried out, his legs buckled. No more, impossible to go on. Where am I now...? Who...? I...? Who is *I*? Who *am* I?

An astonishing thought! – A surprise! – The man grasped his mind in his hand.

Who am I?

But his mind is silent... He has no memory...

What's my name? – What do I look like? Where have

The House of a Thousand Floors

I come from?... My God, I must have had a name in this world... but what was it... what was it?

The pain boring into his temples when he asks that question. If he remembers, everything will become clear and this staircase will disappear... what was it?

More floors stacked up on top of one another, deaf and blind, each with a sun in the ceiling, an electric globe made of milky glass.

II

A terrifying discovery · Hands · Face?
· What was written in the notebook
· The possibility of being a detective · Princess Tamara

For the second time during that frantic flight up, the man stopped in his tracks. Woe! – Horror! – In the white corner of one of the floors is a small pile of white crumbling bones. A fitfully twisted spine snakes through them like a piece of hose. – And, tossed in the corner, the fragment of a cracked human skull. Above the sad heap of bones, at the height of a kneeling man, initials are carved into the wall – . – and five horizontal lines below the initials.

What did it mean? – Someone had hurtled up this staircase before me... S.M. got as far as here and collapsed. He died on his knees, having carved a sign to mark his grave! Five lines... Had he been lost here for five days? Did he take five hours to die?

The running man shivered in terror. Away! Away from here! But where to? There are only two directions: up or down! – Up, then... Stairs and more stairs. The red carpet pierces through his brain like a hot wire. – When was all this going to end? – Ah, if only I knew who I was! I must remember, despite this pain crushing my temples! – Memory! What happened to my memory? – The past, memories, terrible pain! – Who am I?

Then, suddenly, hands. Yes, these are my hands… and I might remember when I see my face. – White hands with long, narrow fingers, the palms speckled with a pink rash. White coat sleeves, sleeves of a silk shirt, white trousers, white canvas shoes… and my face? How will I recognise myself?

The man covered his face with both hands, wanting to grasp his likeness with the nerve ends in his fingertips, the shape of his face – was it handsome or ugly, old or young?… A nose, mouth, hair – was it black or was it, at the same time, also white?

All of a sudden, his blindly groping right hand seized something hard in the inside pocket of his coat – a small notebook. And, on the first page, in unfamiliar handwriting:

> I. Walk through Mullerdom and explore all its floors. Penetrate the bricked-up areas.
> II. Export/import company Universe – star travel. Is it a scam?
> III. The miraculous metal called solium, used to build spaceships for travel to the stars. Is there any truth in this?
> IV. Who is Ohisver Muller? The benefactor of mankind or a vampire? Why is he hiding from the world?
> V. Unexplained kidnappings of beautiful women. – Princess Tamara. Where have they all disappeared to?

The man wondered, am I a detective? Are these the tasks I have been charged with? The main points of a problem to be solved? But how can I work if I've lost my memory?!

He continued leafing through the notebook. There! Three small newspaper cuttings have fallen out. The first one contains the following news item:

Escape or kidnapping?

Tonight, Princess Tamara disappeared from her bedroom, together with her companion Ellie. It is suspected that she has been kidnapped and flown to the Isle of Pride, site of the notorious Mullerdom. But we cannot rule out the possibility that she may have run away since even the princess had herself recently become consumed with desire to travel to the stars. At the same time, her jewellery worth five million has gone missing.

The second cutting reads:

Detective expedition

The detective expedition has just returned from Mullerdom with no results. According to information provided by the offices of the Universe Company, the princess and her companion left for star L4 in the Swan Galaxy. It is worth mentioning that the fare for one person to travel to this lucky star is 250 mulldors or 796,000 of our crowns.

Jan Weiss

And another scrap of paper with a very short item:

The famous detective Petr Brok

has just been charged with the task of finding the princess.

Finally, on the last pages of the notebook, he finds the following list, written in pencil:

> 1. Anna Marton, prima ballerina of the National Opera, 24 March.
> 2. Eva Saratov, model, disappeared from the Artists' Ball minutes after having been declared Queen of the Ball at midnight on 7 April.
> 3. Luna Kori, banker's daughter, disappeared from the Moria Palace in Venice on 30 July.
> 4. Sula May, film star, kidnapped from her villa on 8 September.
> 5. Dora O'Brien, the most beautiful woman in Paris, disappeared from the Bois de Boulogne on 24 October, along with her car.
> 6. Kaja Barard, actress at the Royal Theatre, disappeared after the first act of the opera *The End of the World* on 3 December.

III

*The secret of the first mirror · The house of a thousand floors
· The man who had lost his memory · At last a door in the marble
· News about Muller*

And there was something else the man found in his breast pocket: a sealed letter addressed to –

Petr Brok!

He almost broke the seal when he noticed a warning written in red on the back of the envelope:

Attention! Do not open! This letter can only be opened in front of the first mirror!

What did it mean? Am *I* that detective, Petr Brok? – But his memory is blank and empty, even when a question is asked, there's no reply... As if life had begun with his awakening on the staircase. – And if he insists and tries to remember, a searing pain starts throbbing somewhere in the centre of his brain, like an abscess full of pus. Perhaps I'll find the solution under the seal, he thinks. Perhaps the letter conceals a magic word that will give me back my past, my memories and recollections, my humanity, *myself*... But where can I find the mirror? – I'll die of exhaustion before I do, of exhaustion, hunger or a broken heart!

In the meantime, there was no choice but to be a detective! Perhaps I was a real detective once! And if I want to be a human being again, I *must* have a name. It's impossible to live in the world without a name! But the mind refuses to remember like a madman resisting a straitjacket. – Very well, then! – I will be Petr Brok, detective, at least until I remember... I will search for the princess! – Since I have no past, let me at least find a future...

And there is something else hidden in the corner of one of his pockets that Brok had not noticed before: a sheet of paper, folded eight times. Petr Brok felt jubilant: the plan of Mullerdom! The house of a thousand floors! And yet, it is not a mere house; it is a huge city under a single roof. And I am meant to penetrate this labyrinth? Find Muller, the master of this city? Find the princess on one of these thousand floors? A formidable task for someone with no memory! Or have I been rid of my past so I can dedicate myself fully and single-mindedly to my mission, with my every nerve and every thought? But how can I get there? His pockets gave him no more clues.

Petr Brok set out again on his exhausting journey. He continued climbing the stairs, determined and with no respite; and the floors passed by endlessly, with no sign of

The House of a Thousand Floors

hope. Does this colossus rise to the sky? No windows and no doors. The red carpet becomes unbearable.

An idea crossed Brok's mind: what if there's a secret door hidden in the wall? He started touching the walls with his palms, knocking on them, but the smooth marble panels, uniform, without a single gap, responded with a monotonous, cold hard sound. He ran one floor up and tried the panels again, one by one. His progress was slow. He counted the floors. He should have done that from the beginning, from the moment he woke up. Why didn't he? Because at that point he didn't know yet that he was a detective sent to uncover the great secret of Mullerdom. Before, there had been horror, the chaotic flight of a frightened mind. But now, now he needed to think carefully about every step. Count the floors! How many had he climbed? Thirty? Fifty? They were gone! But let's start from the beginning! Let me measure Mullerdom, albeit from the middle. One... two... three...

As Brok tapped around the walls of the twenty-seventh floor, examining the narrow hairline gaps between the marble slabs, to his astonishment, he discovered a tiny silver knob, almost flush with the surface. First he pressed it. Nothing. Then he took it between his nails and pulled with all his might. And lo and behold! A thin silver needle came out. As soon as he pulled it out, the marble panel yielded and an opening gaped in front of him, leading into darkness. Petr Brok quietly slipped through, closing the door behind him.

He found himself in a pitch black narrow corridor, his head touching the ceiling, his palms feeling the walls on both sides. Slowly, he inched his way forwards. After a few steps, he saw a thin luminous thread hanging in the depth of darkness. When he reached it, he realised it was a narrow gap in the wooden boarding marking the end of the corridor. He pressed his eye to it and saw a small grey room with no windows. A table with a jug, a chair, a bare light bulb and a bed with an iron frame. An old man was sitting on the bed, staring into the light.

Petr Brok watched him for a long while, leaning his forehead against the boards. But the old man didn't move. Then, suddenly, as he pressed his head against the wall, Brok heard the click of a lock and the wall opened. It was a door without a handle. Before he knew what was happening, the detective stumbled into the room.

The old man started and raised his hands against him with a cry.

"Forgive me for disturbing you," said Brok, "Greetings!"

"How did you get here?" whimpered the old man, his chin quivering with fear.

"I came up the staircase. Thank God I found you!"

"Up the staircase?" marvelled the old man. "Are you a human being?"

"What do you think? Don't you like the look of me?"

"I can't see you," said the old man and touched his eyelids with his fingertips. "I'm blind."

And he was! Only now did Brok notice that the man's watery blue pupils quivered in his eyes like frog's spawn.

"Poor you!" he said. And then he asked out of the blue: "And how is Mr Muller?"

The old man hunched his shoulders and an expression of terror passed across his face.

The House of a Thousand Floors

"Our generous benefactor and provider, God and master of the earth and the stars…" he started muttering a confused prayer.

"Why have you been imprisoned here?" asked Brok.

"Be quiet!" whispered the old man in panic, covering his mouth with his hand. "He is all-knowing. Omnipresent. He can hear everything."

"Well, let's have a look at him. What are you afraid of? Death? Or is there something worse that could happen to you? If I succeed in my mission, at least you will die free."

"Give me your hand," said the old man, and then he exploded with hatred and rage: "If you can, Sir, turn this damned house into ashes and dust."

Petr Brok was overcome with curiosity and started pressing him: "Talk to me, tell me everything! Why is this insane house of a thousand floors standing here? What happens inside it? Who is Muller?"

"Sir, how come you don't know? Are you not omnipotent like Him? You've come up the staircase! Are you not the one we've been waiting for? Who *are* you then?"

"Don't ask me. I myself know nothing, except that I have a mission and I will fulfil it. And I am going to face the master of this house, although I don't know him yet and will have to spend a long time looking for him. But do tell me, who is Muller?"

IV

*Who was Muller? · Metal lighter than air
· Human being no. 794 · What did people eat in Mullerdom?*

The old man shook his head. "I don't know. No-body knows. No-one has ever met him. No-one has ever seen his true face. — Some say he's a decrepit old Jew, covered in greasy grime, with red sidelocks. Others have seen a tiny round bald head, attached to a hideous pile of flesh by a double chin. A man who's lost all human form under layers of fat, a stuffed sack that can't move on its own and has to be carried from place to place... Diplomats and bankers with whom he is in contact, however, know a different Muller: a pale aristocrat, around thirty-five, with a monocle and a hanging curled lower lip, as if expressing boundless contempt, and hundreds of years old. Yet others swear he is a white-haired, hunched old man with a face so creased you can't read it any more. Just a pair of tiny grey eyes looking out into the world from among those folds as guilelessly and trustingly as the eyes of a spring baby gazing up from its pram.

But his signature is always the same and it elicits awe and terror wherever it appears. It is thin, as if written with a needle, pointing downwards like a bolt of lightning. It signifies a will, a command, a verdict against which there is no appeal. How many times has Ohisver Muller been murdered? How many bullets have made a hole in his head? How many times has he been drowned, poisoned or lynched by rebelling workers? And yet it is never him! In the end, it always turns out to be one of his secretaries, an *agent provocateur*, a figurine, a double he had planted…"

"And what is solium?" asked Brok as if he had only just remembered the fourth item in his notes. His memory, unburdened by the past, was now working with miraculous speed. To his surprise, he remembered every last detail since he awoke. His brain had absorbed the entire content of the notepad, word for word.

"Solium is a substance discovered on this island deep down below the exploited coal deposits in a new hitherto unknown layer of the Earth's crust closest to its centre. It might be the last skin around its fiery nucleus and solium is an element lighter than air. Once free from soil and impurities, it flies upwards to the sun, never to return.

No-one in the world knows how much solium Muller extracts from his mines. More than iron. More than coal. The world would have to be rebuilt, man would be transformed, and an entirely new way of life would begin on this planet if it were to be used for the benefit of mankind. But Muller jealously guards his mines. He had them covered up, and the only way to reach them is through passages leading from Mullerdom. That's why the world knows nothing about how much solium he owns. – And Muller sells it in minute quantities for extortionate prices, posing as a benefactor. A grain of solium, small as a mote of dust, is sold to universities and wealthy hospitals in exchange for gold worth a fortune. But he himself doesn't use it sparingly! He transforms this substance industrially, turning it into concrete harder than steel and lighter than air. It is this material he has used to build his palace of a thousand floors, his pride, his triumph, his victory. From its pinnacle he surveys the world with a sense of self-importance that reaches even higher than a thousand floors.

Mullerdom has no windows or doors. It's hard to enter and even harder to escape from. It has no connection with the world it has sprung from. This is how Muller guards his vile secret…"

The old man fell silent.

"Tell me who you are," Brok insisted. "Why are you imprisoned here? Aren't you already a prisoner of your blindness? What's your name?"

The old man showed his palms. They were branded with the number 794.

"I have no other name except this number. I come from the eighth brigade of workers who completed eight hundred floors of Mullerdom. Everyone who built this accursed tower went blind within five years. Solium, contained in the concrete, radiates in the sun and damages the human eye. Our entire hundred-floor colony is occupied by blind men, Mullerdom's former builders and bricklayers."

"What do they feed you here?"

The old man pointed to the table. Next to a jug of water was a small cube, wrapped in cellophane marked with the brand name Okka. No bigger than a cube of sugar.

Brok unwrapped it and tasted it with the tip of his tongue: ash, wood, stone... It had no taste.

"This is our breakfast, lunch and dinner. Pressed extract of the nutrients required by the human body for one day. And there's something else in these cubes, something Muller puts in intentionally to suppress our male desires. He wants to destroy in us the miraculous juice that makes men desire women and women men, that turns the surface of the human body with all its protrusions and folds into an island of pleasure where our dreams about a lost paradise come true. — We don't know what love is, and that's why our days are endless and there's no future for us except death. We have no sense of taste, we feel no hunger and we have no wishes or dreams, save for one: an amazing longing that torments us and that not even God Muller can take away from us. A longing for death! Every awakening brings with it terror and our whole day is steeped in our desire for bed, for sleep, for death. Thousands and thousands desire it. One single quiet, dreamless night from which we would never wake up..."

"And you can't leave this place?"

"Where would I go?" asks the old man. "The darkness is everywhere. And even if I could see, I would not run away. What awaits you on the staircase is death by starvation..."

"And where does this door lead to?" asked Brok, who had been examining the room.

"To the corridor. There's an iron grille at the end of it which leads to the fifth sector."

"And what is there?"

V

*West-Wester, the city of adventurers · Gedonia, the city of bliss
· How pleasure is produced in Gedonia*

"West-Wester has attracted adventurers from all over the world. Merchants and traders selling everything from old rags and candles to human souls, virtue and blood, from carpets and gods to face powder and innocence – they've all come here in search of fortune. Agents, spies, layabouts, thieves, gamblers, provocateurs, scabs, traitors, madmen, murderers, an entire army of crooks and criminals offer services of all kinds. Their wealth is measured by floors: the lower the floor, the greater their wealth. The higher they climb, the harder life gets. None of them are satisfied with the floor they're living on. Depending on how well they're doing in business, this riff-raff either seep down or rise up, but, of course, only within the limits of the one hundred floors allocated to them. – So that's West-Wester. Here, once a week, you can drink half a mulldor of your pension courtesy of the generous Muller. Life is hard in these parts for those who can see, let alone for the blind ones. He always dupes us…"

Jan Weiss

Brok remembered his map, the city taking up the fifth one hundred floors. It occurred to him that he could find someone among these adventurers who might be able to show him the way straight to Muller. But it was the lower section of his map that attracted him most, the area called Gedonia. Brok asked the old man about it and he was more than willing to talk.

"Gedonia is a crystal city located on the second hundred floors of Mullerdom. This is where he spends most of his time, surrounded by an entourage of agents, ambassadors, diplomats, financiers and generals. There are halls and dens where, as they say, it's possible to find eternal bliss in this life. This sector is cleverly bricked up and accessible only to a small cohort of selected protégés and sycophants.

Here, physical and mental bliss is produced by chemical and mechanical means, with all manner of pleasures to torture the body and soul to death. – The five existing senses were not capable of encompassing all this stimulation, and so, through all these pleasures, five new senses have been discovered. Physical ecstasy is achieved by using various balsams and concoctions, pills and ointments, massages, injections and operations during which parts of organs and glands are removed from the body, veins are ligated, nerves are shortened. They say that a new pleasure has been found in sneezing, intensified to a catastrophic level by an operation and ending in stupendous death. Titillating showers and baths bring about delightful itching all over the body. There are cults of yawning and tickling, taken to heights that become unbearable.

And when all the stimulants fail, when bodies collapse in exhaustion, drained of every last drop of energy, that's when all the lights go out and a period of rest begins. – Muller himself decides whether it should be day or night in Gedonia because not even the sun has any power in Mullerdom.

The architect who had planned and constructed these divine dens behind innocent walls was himself walled up by Muller in one of the many strange alcoves. Only Muller has a plan of the entire walled-in heaven in his hands. He knows all the secret doors and corridors, unexpected exits through invisible gates opened by hidden mechanisms. These lead into theatres, palaces, churches and even bedrooms. A ceiling rosette with a chandelier hanging down from it, a painting of the crucified Christ on a church altar, a raised parquet in a bedroom floor – these are the heavenly gateways of God Muller through which he can listen, sneak into a room, surprise someone, appear at the right time and then disappear again without a trace."

"And what is there above you?" asked Brok. On his plan, these floors were covered with question marks.

"Hospitals, poorhouses and almshouses where they go to die."

"And above those?"

"Lunatic asylums, jails, dungeons, torture rooms…"

"And above those?"

"Crematoria."

"And then?"

"That's where they keep building… forever… floor upon floor, with no respite, with no end. The city only grows upwards, there's a need for more and more rooms, and we're being pushed up as if by a piston. At moving time, Mullerdom resembles a riotous ant hill. These are days of terror and insanity. The administration, located on fifty floors above Gedonia, is unable to contain the panic that prevails among the inhabitants of Mullerdom at that time."

VI

*The young old man · What the mirror told Brok
· At the end of the corridor · The state of 'dispersion'*

Brok took the old man's hand. Then he remembered his envelope.

"Is there a mirror here, by any chance?"

The old man shook his head sadly.

"What use is a mirror to a blind man? I've been looking into darkness for ten years now."

"How old are you, grandpa?"

"Thirty-three."

Brok looked at the young old man with surprise. Not thirty-three, but eighty years of misery and desperation were carved into his face.

"This is what everyone who lives on Ohisver Muller's cubes looks like."

Petr Brok suddenly had an idea and made a quick decision.

"That's enough! I think I can find a way to get to see the face of your god!"

The old man's eyes filled with tears.

"You're strong; you came up the staircase. I've been

waiting for this door to open for *ten years*. For it is only through here that someone stronger than Muller can come. Lord, make me and my brothers human again! Give us names instead of numbers, food instead of cubes; give us love, desire and dreams! Release us from this prison and give the sun back to those who thought they'd lost it forever!"

"I promise," said Brok and their hands met. And that was when Brok felt the weight of his task. Was he really strong enough to stand up to Muller? And how would he penetrate the forbidden floors without being found?

And again, he remembered the envelope. – Yes, hidden in the envelope was the power that he knew about and that he would recognise in himself when he stood in front of the first mirror. – "Where can I find a mirror?" he asked once more as the old man led him along a long corridor with doors on both sides.

"There's a cage at the end of the corridor," said the old man. "It's a high-speed lift that will take you down to West-Wester. Behind the cage is an alcove. On the wall of this is a polished plate as smooth and cold as a snake. I don't know if it's a mirror. But when I stand in front of it, I feel as if my blindness is staring back at me... I don't know. It may just be glass."

They approached the lift. Brok trembled with anticipation. – They went round the cage, and behind it, below a sad little lamp, there was indeed the gleaming surface of a clear mirror.

Brok hurried ahead and, with the envelope in his hand, he approached the mirror and looked at himself.

A cry of surprise escaped him!

The House of a Thousand Floors

He stood upright. He waved his hands. He jumped up and down. – He gave various signs that he was there, a human being standing in front of a mirror, but all in vain; the mirror could not see him, the mirror ignored him.

The mirror was blank.

The wall opposite was faithfully reflected in its surface but the man who stood between it and the mirror could not see himself. What kind of damn mirror was this? A mirror that did not show your reflection? And then, Brok saw the old man hobbling towards him in this miraculous pool. – Lo and behold! The old man was reflected in the polished rectangle right down to the last wrinkle, all on his own! A wild idea exploded in Petr Brok's mind. He eagerly broke the red seal, unfolded the half sheet of white paper and read:

Of my own free will and at my own risk, I have lent my body to Master Oskar Eril to use it for what is known as the 'dispersion experiment', so that I could in this manner and form (i.e., being invisible) infiltrate all areas of Mullerdom and uncover its suspicious secrets. And if the terrible conjectures are confirmed, I will murder the man who calls himself Ohisver Muller at once, having been authorised to do so by the secret session of the judicial congress of USW (United States of the World) on the Island of Last Hope – Consumed with a burning desire for truth and justice, and for the salvation of humankind, I make this sacrifice without claim to any reward whatsoever, and without fear of the consequences I had been warned of.
Signed Petr Brok

Underneath, the following lines were written by a different hand:

> *I confirm by my signature that the effects of the state of dispersion will fade away after exactly thirty days.*
> *Signed Oskar Eril*

Only now did Petr Brok begin to understand his amazing power! He grabbed the old man around the waist and spun him around in a crazy dance, in the first wave of joy he had felt since waking up.

The old man then touched the surface of the mirror with his finger and stepped back, frightened.

"Oh, I fear the mirror under my hand. Mirrors respond even to the blind... A mirror never stops seeing."

"Grandpa," shouted Brok, "you wouldn't be able to see me anyway, even if you had a thousand eyes. No-one can see me...!"

Brok couldn't get enough of his invisibility. He skipped in front of the mirror, tapped it, breathed on it and stroked it — but to no avail! As if the mirror grew tired of receiving and giving back human shapes. No! It was rather as if it had suddenly rebelled, and, quite selectively, refused to reflect Petr Brok. And he was far from being angry! On the contrary, he thought: What power I have! Like a god. I can do anything. I can perform miracles not even Jesus Christ could dream of. I will surprise the world imprisoned in this skyscraper. Mullerdom is now mine!

He hastened to bid the young old man farewell and stepped into the cage of the lift. As soon as the iron grille shut behind him, he felt a shock. The lift started descending fast and he felt as if he were falling into an abyss. He closed his eyes. The headlong plunge gave him vertigo. His temples began to pound. Then Petr Brok lost consciousness.

VII

Again the dream with the yellow lamp · Windows and people · The inn at the end of the world · The dream merchant

As he kept falling, to his surprise, that heavy oppressive dream came back. — A yellow lamp with a flame flickering anxiously inside a skull. It doesn't light anything except itself and a yellow circle of dust swirling around it. He dreams that he is lying curled up in a damp, freezing building, his head between his knees. He pushes aside the grey cocoon he is wrapped in. — As his eyes become accustomed to the dim light, as if through a veil, he can see cracked wooden beams crossing above his head unfathomably in all directions. On a suspended platform, people are lying in a tight row, left side up, warming each other in their laps. — But he is no longer a link in this chain; he is lying opposite, by a broken window covered in white frost. — He is cold. He pulls the cocoon back over his head, curls up and wraps himself up in darkness that could be both night and day...

Petr Brok woke up. — With a start, he opened his eyes, and the tormenting illusion disappeared. How long had he been sleeping? He stood up in the lift cage and immediately remembered the previous day. He eagerly grasped the grille as if he wanted to preserve this reality that had preceded that terrible dream with a yellow lamp in the middle of a hollow skull. He felt a painful desire in anticipation of what was to come. With astonishment, he remembered that he was invisible and stepped out of the lift.

He walked through a narrow passage, down several steps, opened a cast iron gate – and found himself in a street. Two rows of buildings, shop signs and pavements. Only one thing was missing here, something that belongs to every street, although nobody notices it… the sky. Instead of the sky, there was a high vaulted ceiling made from a single piece of glass. Underneath it a massive globe glowed, white and unbearable like the sun at its zenith.

Windows and people. – Endless rows of windows and people. Windows that were silent and windows that shout, windows surprised and tearful, enigmatic, yawning with boredom, windows, windows, windows – beckoning, luring, laughing and weeping. – And among them a multi-coloured, effervescent crowd of people rushing in all directions, circulating ceaselessly, a mixture of all human races. The colours of their clothes, skin, eyes and hair all mingle; voices come out of thousands of mouths as if from the pipes of an organ that had escaped from a burning cathedral.

And just as the sky and sun above their heads are both fake, it seems to Brok that all those people, strutting and shouting, have something phoney and monstrously artificial about them. The faces of the men are clean-shaven or covered with beards of various shapes and styles, but many of these appear to Brok to be false, glued on. –

Some of these people are ostensibly enjoying themselves, laughing for no apparent reason. Others are hurrying somewhere with an expression of anxiety or even terror in their faces. A Chinaman over there is stealthily sneaking below the windows, following someone. And over here, a criminal is on the prowl, with a small black patch over his eye. – A shot sounds behind one of the doors but no-one pays attention. A sailor with a pock-marked face, wearing a black and yellow T-shirt, staggers drunkenly, belting out a lewd song. Three men with bare torsos and black masks covering their faces, arrogantly swagger down the street, daggers behind their belts. The crowd parts in front of them. A row of figures with purple hoods over their heads and round holes for eyes file down the street. – The windows of dancing halls open wide with yellow laughter… Li-la-lo-lu, says a Japanese woman, an ornamental needle stuck in her hairdo, like a dagger piercing a black heart. She is walking arm in arm with a gangster who amuses himself by tripping up old men. As he bares his red-stained teeth, he has just kicked a legless beggar and sent him sprawling over a sewer grate.

A black shop sign screams:

⚒ **DIAMONDS AND COAL** ⚒
FOR SALE!

A hawker wheezes:

'OVA' cube is **THE BEST!!!**

Jan Weiss

A green and black banner:

THE INN | AT THE END OF THE WORLD

A small window opens:

No more despair!
Buy KOKA!

Grey days will become rosy!
Cowards will be transformed into heroes!
Defeat will turn into victory!

Violet face powder like a mask on women's faces. Gleaming white teeth, black squares of windows, jingle bells, and, under the red drop of a light bulb, a woman throws around penetrating words, her crude gestures suggesting that she is the seller, the shop and the merchandise all in one:

> "Hurry along, young and old.
> Before you pass me by
> Look at my face!
> Notice my hair,
> Appreciate the colour of my eyes!
> Feel the firmness of my breasts
> For free…
> Touch my calves
> Hard as the rails

The House of a Thousand Floors

Along which passion speeds!
I am burning, I am burning
For eight argents
I will torture you to death with my love…"

And opposite her, a man with a red forked goatee sits over a rickety table covered with small boxes. Surrounded by several gawkers, he shouts:

Buy dreams!
Guaranteed quality goods!
They last a whole night!

Dreams about gold!
Become a millionaire for one night!
Buy my "Gold Dream"!
Protected trademark!

A single AGA pill
before you go to sleep will guarantee
a night full of love, kisses and embraces
Instructions for use

Special offer! Rosy dreams!
Try one and you'll come back for more!
No side effects!

Do you want to travel to exotic places?
See palm trees, caravans, savages,
tigers and monkeys?
Buy our EXOTICS tablets

Jan Weiss

Fall asleep on your back with an ARO pastille under your tongue
and you'll experience
a plane journey to the sun!

Try an ORA pill
to experience
a hurricane for one night
and survive it in the safety
of your bed

Are you afraid to journey to the stars?
Is star travel beyond your means?
Dreams can bring you this adventure!
Buy my Stardream for five argents!
Beware of fakes!

Gigantic signs, moving neon patterns repeating themselves until they make you go mad; advertisements everywhere: on banners, walls, windows, doors, on people's backs and even on their faces. – Paper, colours, glass and human mouths all scream at Brok from all directions, filling his eyes and ears. He had been walking on for a long while, not stepping aside for anyone, amused at the sight of the unsuspecting passers-by who collided with him and jumped, their faces transformed by surprise and terror. He veered to the right following the road. Then he realised that he had been walking in a circle and had returned to his starting point. Only then did he notice the narrow, winding streets running from the main circular road onto which the crowds slowly trickled. Metal walls rusty with dampness, windows muzzled with curved grilles. Some streets were so narrow that you could touch the walls with both hands. And there were streets like mountain passes where the walls almost touched and people had to squeeze through sideways, holding their breath and drawing their bellies in.

VIII

*The shops in Tiger Street · Hotel Eldorado
· A clean-handed joint venture · Revolution in Mullerdom*

Petr Brok entered one of these side streets. The glass tiles underfoot were covered in dirt. Some were cracked or broken, letting in light. Through one of these chinks in the floor, Brok could see the same crowds milling around below, phosphorescent colours flashing, and he could even hear the shouting of street vendors.

This street, too, was full of various shop signs, but more discreet and not as loud. The more modest the sign, the better the shop and more sought after the owner. A dirty business card stuck on the door, a small notice in the window, an enamel plaque the size of a palm. There was no more shouting; here, the signs spoke in suggestive whispers.

> — OPIUM —
> The best quality

> **HYPNOSIS** here

Jan Weiss

Arpag Merle alchemist

• IMMA •
painless death

ELIXIR R-A
extends life according to your wishes

Fr. IPS forged IOUs
signatures
counterfeit money

MAGIC SPELLS
SANDOR, SABATH

Joe MINA
petty thefts, pick-pocketing, etc., inconspicuous

D R O P S
eternal oblivion

G e n t l e m e n !
Buy only rays
GGGGGGGGGGGGG

SCHWARTZ and Co.,
WWWWW production

Ko-Son-Ma
kidnappings

The House of a Thousand Floors

Behind a window among small bottles is a metal sign:

POISON SELLER

On a rusty wall scribbled with chalk:

GARPONA lets blood all day! Discreetly!

Painted letters running down a wooden plank:

CHULKOV, madness

Across a dark narrow street, there is a wire stretched from wall to wall, supporting a swaying signboard with a painted dagger and the words:

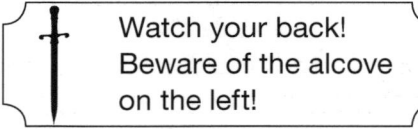

Watch your back!
Beware of the alcove
on the left!

Further down, a warped sign hangs sideways above a door. The staggering letters, as if written by a drunk's finger dipped in mud, announce:

Petr Brok decided to visit this dubious hotel. For one thing, he was tired and he also wanted to have a good look at the clientele. He entered a small dark hall smelling of mice, sweaty laundry and something else, something quite unbearable. A door led from the hall into a large room painted in gaudy colours like a bar. The ceiling was fitted with a round convex glass, the purpose of which was not clear to Brok.

There were people sitting at the round table, but Brok had no time to observe the company that had gathered there because precisely at that moment someone said the word 'revolution', a word that makes as strong an impact on the ear as the sight of blood makes on the eye.

"Revolution!" shouted a man with a double-pointed black goatee. "The slaves have risen in the factory district! The uprising has already spread over eighty floors! It all started in the Omega Cube factory, with someone called Vítek of Vítkovice, a slave driver who betrayed our Great Muller. He secretly organised resistance and now he's calling for the entire world to be saved from Muller's clutches. He wants to bring the slaves to power, and replace them in the machine halls and mine shafts with aristocracy from the lower floors.

The workers from the Omega Cube factory were soon joined by another 1,980 men from the chemical plant, 260 from the mint factory, 400 from the foundry, 5,380 from the gas works and 250 from the liqueur factory. They've already smashed their way through into the City of Darkness, where they gained the support of the population with their call to establish a republic and their promise that even the blind will be represented in its government. They want to use them to form a terrible vanguard, like a wall. If they manage to penetrate the City of Darkness, there's a danger they'll open the prisons located on the upper floors. What's worse is they're also breaking through downwards, destroying machinery and equipment. They've plundered offices on floors 690 to 700 and they're making their way to floor 680 where the warehouses start. This means they are only 60 floors away from the provisions stores. Of course, they're finding it difficult to make their way through the hard ceilings made of solium concrete. Luckily, the lifts have stopped working; the power plants are located in the first zone and the supply was immediately cut off. The main staircase is blocked with barricades and it'll take them months to break through those since their equipment is so basic.

But our Great Muller doesn't want them on his conscience, although he could easily exterminate them with gas. He believes that it will be possible to convince them to give up. That's why he sent me here, to West-Wester to hire several experts so we can infiltrate the movement and poison it from inside, bring chaos into the revolutionary ranks, and, above all, get rid of Vítek of Vítkovice who is the soul of this palace revolt and the brains behind it. Mind you, Muller has tried to bribe them with gold – but to no avail..."

IX

*Garpona · Mr Perker · Poisons · KAWAI serum · SIO gas
· Glass lenses on the temples of the blind man*

"Maybe with a dagger?" asked a rectangular man everyone called Garpona. He had no arms and served himself with his feet.

"You've heard him, the gracious Muller doesn't ask for blood," muttered a man with an obscenely large purple nose, like a massive bunch of grapes, which took up most of his face and it seemed to Brok that it continued growing and ripening as he watched.

"I've got goods that are tried and tested and have proven their efficacy a thousand times, which I administer myself with guaranteed success. If you like, the victim will die of a heart attack. One drop of poison U will have a lethal effect on the brain. A dose of G will bring on cancer. I also have O cigars . Or a milligram of E in a glass of milk…"

"I work exclusively with bulk orders," a blind man with a deep baritone voice interrupted the man with the big nose. His eyelids were stitched together, which gave his face a terrible sense of calm. But on his temples he had two metal cases, each fitted with a sharp gleaming lens, like the eyes of a predatory bird.

"The revolution could be destroyed with my germs… The Great Muller knows about me…"

"The slaves' turn will come but, first of all, we must take out Vítek! – Not kill him, do you understand? His body can go on living. It's his soul we have to destroy, his soul or his brain!"

"Inject his brain with KAWAI serum and he'll go mad," a short man with a double hunchback advised.

"Inhaling SIO gas will turn him into an old man overnight," added a decrepit trembling old man, bald as a coot. "He'll spend the rest of his life dying in senility. The apparatus can be placed in the bedroom unnoticed. It's like a toy, a little rubber ball that's found its way into a corner…"

"The best dagger, the best poison, the best serum, the best gas – are eyes!" a yellowish face spelled out cautiously but emphatically, its round black eyes glittering with white hot squares.

"Very well," said the agent and took out a writing pad. "I'm going to make a note of your names: Mr Garpona – dagger, Mr Perker – poison, Mr Schwartz – Sio, Mr Orsag – bacteria, Mac Doss – hypno, Sudar Chulkov – Kawai. All of you come to 8 Orange Street on the 274th floor tomorrow and bring everything you've just described to me with you. An aerolift will transport you to the top of Mullerdom, and from there you'll be able to easily penetrate the heart of the revolution and mix in with the plebs… The Great Muller will then reward you according to the success of your mission…"

The House of a Thousand Floors

"To hell with it!" cursed the handless assassin when the agent left. "No work to speak of! I might just as well stick my dagger into a pile of manure!" – He was fiddling with his feet under the table and then again on top of it. Then he wiped his brow with the sole of one foot and loudly clicked the toes of the other.

"You smell of blood, brother," the master of poisons muttered and, with an expression of great satisfaction, blew his nose on the ground. Then he wiped his unbearable nose with a red handkerchief, adding: "Our work is clean… no blood on *our* hands."

"Who says I only work with a dagger?" asked the assassin. "Pay me twenty mulldors more and I'll strangle him with hands as clean and pure as a bride's." He slid his feet out of his slippers under the table and spread his long white toes to show he meant business.

"We're both amateurs," said the poison master, "Let Mr Orsag tell us how he fed his germs to a whole army of miners."

The blind man did not deign to reply but the sinister lenses on his temples flashed as he turned to the big-nosed man.

"And what about Mr Schwartz?" Big Nose persisted, this time questioning the tremulous little old man. "How many people did you age overnight?"

"I work downstairs, in the financial district," lisped the toothless Schwartz. "I've just installed a small device on the eighth floor of the second zone, in young Gerel's bedroom. He's the son of that top loan shark who sold Alaska and the African colonies to Muller. Adria, his niece, wants to inherit his wealth. In a week, Gerel Junior will be older than his father. Another one, Sir Moru, the biggest shareholder of the Universe Company, is ageing with every step he takes."

"And is that your doing, too?" Big Nose wondered. "They say he he's got a lot of problems."

"That's right... His shares will end up in the hands of a man whose name I cannot reveal. I believe that *I* have done the most for our benefactor, our Lord..."

"I'm not sure what you mean when you say 'the most', my dear Schwartz," Double Hunchback piped up, then turned to the man with the burning eyes. "Mac Doss, our Doctor of Hypnotism, is new among us and has not yet heard my story... eeh... if it were not for me, our good Father and Lord would be finished."

X

Astronomer Galio, master of the stars
· The first ship to travel into space · Muller's hunger for the stars
· How Galio became a big zero
· Sudar Chulkov, the king of fifty thousand stars

The hunchback raised two fingers to the convex glass eye in the ceiling: "I'm telling the truth. Let Great Muller be my witness if He happens to be kindly looking down on His humble servants. I rid Him of an enemy who would have sucked up all the miraculous fluid that gushes like a fountain underneath Mullerdom, from which He drinks… Today, everyone knows this… clack, clack – he was old Galio, the star merchant. – His son, who now resides on three floors in the third zone, is a mere amateur compared to his father. Muller lets him trade with worthless, discarded stars: burning stars, stars covered in snow or comets that fly by and never come back. No-one wants them; they're useless merchandise – but old Galio, what a genius! Meh! He set up an astronomy observatory on a small island in Polynesia and performed miracles with a single grain of solium. The natives made him their king and he united about ten islands under his rule. That was when the Great Muller travelled the seas buying up the remaining parts of our world. He visited old Galio in his observatory that doubled as his royal residence. When asked what he wanted in exchange for his small island, the sly old man said modestly: "The night sky!"

He would not accept a speck of gold! Meh, meh! Our good Lord Muller saw this as the whim of an old eccentric who was in love with his celestial jewels he observed night after night. It was as if He got the islands for free. The stars belong to no-one, not even Muller Himself, but if the silly old man wanted them, why wouldn't He sell them to him? If he wants to be a fool, let him be one! They signed a contract: Muller became the master of ten Polynesian islands, while Galio became the master of all the stars. One had a pig in a poke, the other a bird in the bush! Chirp! Chirp!! Not just one, but billions of birds who flew to him on clear nights, always in the same flock.

What Muller didn't know then was that it would become possible to use solium to make spacecraft that would crisscross the universe like a swarm of mosquitoes! By then, he had long forgotten about his contract, when the first swallow set out and returned weighed down with untold riches from nine stars. Universe Company was founded, opening up new inexhaustible sources of fabulous wealth. And that was when old Galio reminded Muller about the contract! It turned out that all the stars discovered by Universe already belonged to Galio because of the contract signed by Muller himself. And Our Lord realised how much the ten little islands had cost him... Galio became the master of all the

The House of a Thousand Floors

stars, while Muller owned just one, the one on which he stood. Li-li-li! Meh, meh! – Fairytale riches, exotic fruits, new metals and unknown precious stones – all of this belonged to Galio according to that damned old contract! Chirp, chirp, chirp…

And so our great benefactor had to buy the conquered stars back from Galio one by one… His Highness simply couldn't bear the thought that someone else could be the master of every newly discovered star, and that the star could carry any other name than the one he himself bestowed on it, just as he could not accept that any contract bearing his signature would be anything but sacrosanct. And so as fast as new stars were being discovered, Galio was selling and Muller was buying. But Galio's stock was endless. Meh, meh! And Muller kept paying and paying, until things went so far that he had to start selling parts of the world to satisfy his desire to own the stars… And the most bizarre thing was Galio categorically refused to accept riches from any other planet, no matter how valuable. He only accepted goods produced on our good old Earth. And what did he do with all that wealth, you might ask? – He began giving Muller's gold away to the poor. Cities, islands, mines, industrial plants, everything Muller gave him in exchange for his stars, he would give it all to workers and the poor… They called him the Liberator!

Ah, what a clever plan this was – to destroy Ohisver Muller who, disgraced and almost destitute, was ready to leave the Earth and move out to one of his stars…

And then – chirp chirp – at the last minute when Muller was close to bankruptcy and in the middle of selling Mullerdom to Galio who was planning to blow it up –

that's when I started treating Galio's rheumatism. Cluck – cluck! One evening – I remember it as if it were only yesterday – his joints stopped aching and he was in a fine mood. I asked him how many stars he'd already sold to Muller and how many he still had left.

"As many as I had at the beginning," Galio smiled mysteriously. "Even if I sold him a million stars every day, Muller would have to live a million years to acquire a tiny fraction of them all!" Meh, meh!

And that night, when Galio fell asleep, I injected three drops of Kawai under his skin – Chirp, chirp! – Come morning, Galio jumps up: "Pen! Paper! How much money do I have?" He writes down a nine and begins adding zeros. During that first day, he covered ten sheets of paper with zeros. Since then, his brain has turned into a zero-generating machine. All his thoughts revolve around zeros! Miaow!

I could then easily get hold of that cursed contract and pass it on to Muller. And Galio has been living in a lunatic asylum ever since, counting zeros. He himself became one big zero! – And that's the story of how I saved Our Lord Muller! He's still paying for his mistake, mind you, picking up the pieces after all the damage old Galio managed to wreak. – He wanted to make me the Emperor of Bradierra to show his gratitude! – Meh, meh – I declined. He told me to choose any empire, any throne; he asked me whether I wanted to be a king, general or diplomat. I told him that all I wanted was to be allowed to live out my days in Mullerdom, close to him, basking in the reflected glory of His Highness. In the end, he convinced me to accept fifty thousand stars and declared

The House of a Thousand Floors

me the master of all these worlds. — I wanted to travel to one of them, meet my subjects and be crowned. Just one, not all of them, of course! If I were to be crowned every day in one of my kingdoms, I would have to live at least a hundred and thirty-seven years. And then, Ohisver Müller doesn't want me to go anywhere. He keeps begging me to stay close to him in case he needs anything..."

XI

Petr Brok's curiosity and what came of it
· The poison master's nose · Battle in the cube
· Armless Garpona raged more than anyone else

The hunchback fell silent and his eyes moved with curiosity from face to face around the table. – Big Nose blew a sad slow melody of spring hay fever into his purple handkerchief. The blind man's face loomed above the table like a block of marble – but the two lenses on his temples glittered gaily, as if laughing out loud. At least that's how it appeared to Petr Brok. – The armless assassin seemed not to be listening, and he kept his feet busy like a dexterous monkey. He would twiddle his toes under the table and then scrabble around on the table top again. Then he pulled out his dagger with his left foot and threw it towards the ceiling so skilfully that it spun round like a propeller. But before it came down and he caught it with his right foot, he managed to empty his glass. Then he took out a snuff box from the pocket of his waistcoat, sprinkled some green powder on his ankle, drew it all in and sneezed with such force that he woke up the frail old Schwartz, who had meanwhile fallen asleep.

Jan Weiss

Then, when this episode was over and everyone suddenly stopped talking as if overcome with unexpected shyness, Petr Brok spoke. Not because he wanted to reveal himself. He simply had the urge to speak into the hunchback's ear, ask him about something he wanted to know. He would merely whisper his question so that the hunchback would be convinced that it was one of his companions speaking. Brok felt awkward in his invisible state, disadvantaged, isolated, excluded from their trust, dependent on long and fruitless debates that brought him no benefit... He wanted to ask the little hunchback his question, but the others' ears were like monitors camouflaged with tufts of hair. And so he brought his mouth almost to the hunchback's ear and asked in a colourless, quiet voice, as if nothing were amiss: "Tell me, what does the divine Ohisver Muller look like?"

The hunchback froze, his eyes popped out and his jaw dropped at the same time, his face puffed up with shock. To Brok it appeared to stretch momentarily from wall to wall. But it was just an illusion. The hunchback's pale face was back between his shoulders like a wedge driven into a lump of wood. – He jumped up, becoming a head shorter because the legs of the chair were longer than his.

"Which one of you spoke?" he screamed. "I say, who's just spoken?"

The others were surprised. No-one else had spoken since he himself had finished talking!

"I heard a voice! I swear by Lord Muller! "The hunchback raised his right hand towards the round glass in the ceiling. "I'm not lying! Someone is here!"

"Perhaps the Great Muller deigned to...," the poison

master stated humbly and looked up to the ceiling with dread.

"No, no! Someone asked about Muller himself."

"Who?"

"A voice! A voice whispered in my ear!"

"Is that Kawai talking? Have you infected your own brain with madness?"

"*You* are mad, all of you! I swear! By every one of my fifty thousand stars!"

Old Schwartz sympathetically tapped his forehead: as careful as he might have been with his gas, the hunchback himself was probably suffering from dementia.

Meanwhile, Petr Brok sat quietly on the chair vacated by the agent. He felt an enormous power over these human freaks; he could show them if he wanted to. He thought about the revolution on the workers' floors, about Vítek of Vítkovice, about everything these scoundrels were planning, and wondered how he could get rid of them without getting his own invisible hands dirty...

At that moment, he found the poison master's juicy, bottomless nose in front of him, just emptied and already filling up again. This tragic nose had irritated him from the beginning, made him feel almost painful disgust. Unable to bear it any longer, Brok, overwhelmed with hatred for that ghastly nose, picked up a glass and threw it with all his might. – Blood spurted, the poison master floundered. The rest of them jumped up horrified and grabbed their noses.

But this all happened in a matter of seconds and soon the gang came to their senses. They stood with their backs to each other and, in a split second, were all holding revolvers. The black, wide-open eyes of the weapons moved around, aiming into space. A mad crossfire sounded in the cube. There were gunshots, whistling bullets, shattering mirrors and dust rising from all corners.

And the armless Garpona raged more than anyone else. Lying on the table on his back, he pushed himself round with one foot, his dagger in the other stabbing in all directions, looking more like a harpy than a human being.

XII

*The treacherous lenses on the blind man's temples
· Petr Brok was trapped · Escape
· The lift – and the dream again*

Petr Brok shivered. He could have sworn that the sharp lenses on the blind man's temples were staring at him! It was as if his face were made of stone, eyelids stitched together, as still as a sphinx. But the sharply cut lenses, burning inside, were staring straight into Brok's face...

Was it an illusion? Or had he given himself away? Was it possible that the blind man could see him?

Brok got up. The lenses lifted, following his face. Then the blind man touched his temples, adjusting a small serrated ring, as if focusing a microscope. It seemed to Brok that his every movement was captured by these lenses.

Unknown terror passed through his body like ice-cold lightning. His knees buckled. He sat down again and lowered his eyes to the table. Terrified, he looked up to see two black flames burning in the lenses like hot coals. – Then the marble face became hideously distorted, and a hand pointed a finger between his eyes like the barrel of a gun.

Jan Weiss

The blind man screamed: "Here he is! Block the doors! – No shooting! We have to get him alive!"

Armless Garpona leapt to one door, Perker to the other, while the blind Orsag traced Brok's every movement with the barrel of his index finger, approaching him very slowly, circling around him, ready to pounce.

Petr Brok was trapped. He had to fight his way through to one of the doors; otherwise, he was going to fall into their hands. One door was blocked by Big Nose, the other by Garpona, who was balancing on one foot, locking the door with the other. Brok made a move towards the door. Orsag shouted and stood in his way. Brok punched him in the stomach, tripped Garpona up by his single foot, leapt to the door, opened it, rushed through and shut it behind him, all in one split second. Then he raced down a narrow dark alleyway – where to he had no idea...

My God, how many steps he had to run up and down, how many corridors with walls diverging and converging, with undulating ceilings. How many rooms he rushed through, how many spacious halls, dark holes and tiny spaces serving God knows what purpose. At one point, he found himself on a gallery surrounding an empty, dusty hall. Then he crossed a hidden bridge over the abyss of a skylight. – And behind him the stomping of feet like a drum call, growing in number and moving faster and faster. And then more alleyways, steps and arcades, followed by more open spaces...

Brok entered a smooth, shiny cylinder. It was a sewer! No, it was the muzzle of a cannon. No! It was an astronomer's telescope, becoming narrower and narrower... He could only crawl on his knees and soon he would

The House of a Thousand Floors

only be able to wriggle forward, inch by inch, like a caterpillar, until he could go no further... This was the end, the end... But the telescope suddenly ended with a wire mesh. Brok grabbed it and shook it desperately.

Strange! – He could remove the rusty sieve easily, without effort. Petr Brok slipped through and closed it behind him. The floor under his feet began descending. At the last minute, he glimpsed a face with a broken nose behind the mesh. One second longer and it would have been too late.

In the lift, during his endless fall into an abyss, that unbearable sensation caught up with him again. – An intolerable pressure clamped his brain like a vice, until he almost lost consciousness again. The terrible dream returned to torment him. He struggled with all his might to stave off nightmarish monsters, to stop them entering his mind, for fear he might once more fall into that foul subterranean hole where something terrifying was happening inside grey cocoons.

Petr Brok was terrified of these dreams. He felt as if his old body woke up in them, having lost its immateriality. He was reminded of the existence of his old body with all its aches and pains. He was afraid he might perish in one of his dreams before he completed his mission high up there, on one of Mullerdom's thousand floors.

XIII

*Chapter about stars · Planetary trade and industry · Advertising
· Seashell as a talisman*

When Petr Brok recovered his senses, the lift had come to a standstill. His eyelids were still heavy with the dream when he entered a wide crowded arcade. Where was he now? What floor was he on?

How far down did he still have to go to find Muller? Was this perhaps the Tower of Babel?

On both sides, people were lingering in front of splendid altar-like shop windows with their hands in their pockets. Next to the luxury shops were kiosks and stalls where florists, perfume sellers, photographers, antique dealers, junk merchants and many other traders were praising their strange wares loudly. Delicatessen shop windows were odes to plenty, paeans to symmetry, boasting towers, pyramids and garlands made of miraculous fruits, creatures, colourful boxes and tins. These were the goods brought from other planets! Petr Brok read:

**Healing water from
Lake Alpha
on Star M14!**

Jan Weiss

Edible moss from the rainforests of Star C71!
•
**NA-HA powder
from birds' wings from
Z179!**
•
**Perfumes made with tears of angels from
D55!**
•
**Blood of elfin dwarfs
(H70)
to cure monkey disease!**
•
**Hormonal glands of water creatures
– a delicacy on B1!**
•
**Shoes made of the skin of F99 origons
are indestructible!**
•
**Manna from
B64
tastes like almonds!**

Other advertisements offered planetary emigrants various products from home:

**Settlers on
L20
– Seeds of the best quality!
A single seed brings you
a hundred times better harvest!**

The House of a Thousand Floors

ACHA powder
to protect against pink insects on
C71!
You won't regret your purchase.
It'll be money well spent!

•

AZ
astronomical watch
will show you the right time
on any planet!!!

Lower your blood pressure
in Spiral Galaxy
with Spiral balm!

Metal strips, beads, mirrors
and aluminium foil
for natives of K5
will secure their services!!!

Throw LANA chocolate
to erols on Z2!
They'll give you anything
you want in return!

Waterproof umbrellas, coats and tents
to keep out night rain on K86!

Buy SHADE sunglasses
if you want to sleep on S34,
the planet of eternal day!

Jan Weiss

**Buy your insurance
before travelling
to new planetary worlds!**

**Live inhabitants of G5
in PANOPTIKUM OMEGA
will make you laugh till you cry!**

Under a marquee with red and yellow stripes, a seashell vendor displays shells resembling stars, flowers and animals or nothing at all in this world. The vendor holds the seashells up one by one, putting them to his ear, whispering something to them and then again he howls at the crowds in a hoarse voice:

**An IZA seashell
from planet B55
used as a paperweight on your desk
will inspire you when writing letters!**

**An O-RA seashell
from the black lake on
F39
resembles a black swan!
Secretly slip it to your enemy
to make him plagued by failure!**

**Like water lilies
from a frozen star,
A-KA seashells hold the secret
to success in love!**

The House of a Thousand Floors

**U-VA seashells from the star
Albatros
resemble petrified butterflies.
Put one under your pillow and dream of the stars!**

**The NE-O seashell from P44
sounds like a stormy ocean
and will protect you on all your travels
through Mullerdom for ten years!"**

Opposite the seashell vendor stands an art dealer with paintings of fantastic planetary landscapes and cities. Next to him, another vendor hollers, and then another one. Competing with them, the cracking fireworks of advertisements burn stigmata onto the forehead of the night.

XIV

*The terror of darkness · The export and import company
· UNIVERSE – transport to the stars
· Petr Brok can't remember · A Dutch colony on the moon*

Suddenly all the lights went out and the entire space under the glass bell jar exploded with darkness.

A catastrophe!

Maybe the power plant workers had rebelled, too, and joined the revolution. Maybe all the floors had been plunged into darkness, and a terrible, endless night was about to start, full of monsters and blood.

MULLERDOM WITHOUT ANY WINDOWS!

Petr Brok had no time to imagine the horror of it, the horror that would grip this absurd ant hill of Muller's thousand-floor empire – when he was surprised by a great light. – But wasn't Mullerdom a world on its own where Muller himself dictated when it would be day and night? It wasn't the sun, but blazing letters written on the blackboard of the night by an invisible hand.

Jan Weiss

**Buy plots on other planets
with low-interest loans
UNIVERSE COMPANY**

And it continued:

Eternal spring on the shores of star E4

Live a fairytale in the blue valleys of star M21

Become an angel on star R25

**Celestial women of
IKI-LA
long for you**

You can be a king on star J25

**Are you looking for a bride
for a single wedding night?
We recommend U55**

You can live for a thousand years on star P7

**Heavenly drink on the moon
of the fourth star Z22**

You will never die on star P5

Then the ball lit up again and the signs disappeared. Only one remained, bright as the sun, above the entrance to a translucent palace with fluorescent edges and ledges in all the colours of the rainbow. It read:

UNIVERSE

Brok slipped through a door into a large room where the four walls welcomed him with a riot of colours. Paintings and maps covered the walls from floor to ceiling.

Orbit trajectories of suns and stars, the parabolic paths of comets, milky nebulae with names and numbers marking the bodies floating in them. A network of planetary transport where arterial roads in space crossed the trajectories of planets. Diagrams, tariffs, price lists and travel schedules. Models of planetary systems made of glass and metal. Plastic representations of fantastic landscapes overrun with rampant vegetation.

Is this flora or crystals of celestial minerals? Or are these perhaps the inhabitants of these stars? Is this a giants' rainforest or a colony of Lilliputians?

Then Brok stopped short. Among the suspect multi-coloured fairytale shapes that assailed him from all sides, he suddenly saw an image that made him feel as if someone were caressing him with a kind hand. What an unexpected surprise! A piece of – Earth! Squares of cultivated land in familiar colours, hills covered with forests in the background and, above them, blue dissolving into the distance... in the middle of the fields, a small chapel with a red roof and doors with round peepholes.

My God, it's as if I know this landscape from somewhere. It was long, long ago that I used to stand on tiptoe looking into these round eyes of the chapel. The sad scent of the past came wafting out of those round holes, and inside, in the quiet semi-darkness, a saint was standing at the altar. Which saint? And who was that person looking at him? And when? If only he could remember how it all was then! What were the connections? What happened between the chapel and the accursed staircase where he woke up one day, with no memory and no past?

The image of that chapel was somewhere at the back of his mind, having entered through his eyes. If only he could remember! Everything would immediately... But, look! Above the landscape was the sky with three large moons, each a different colour, red, green and orange. Underneath Brok read:

A Dutch colony on the moon III
of Star S1
No need to work.
Nature will work for you!
Native dwarfs will be your servants!

But wasn't discovering the truth the easiest thing in the world for Brok to do? All the doors in Mullerdom were open for him. All the secrets would turn grey before his eyes. All illusions would melt like snow falling into fire.

XV

*The different categories of emigrants · The impoverished millionaire
· The lecherous Lothario · Alva, the missionary
· Abbé Lar · Frank Farani*

A swarm of people are milling around a glass partition with a row of small windows. It is enough to stand by one of the windows and listen.

"I used to be a millionaire," says a red-haired man in tattered clothes. "Las Abela, have you heard of me? I used to own factories making engines, cars and aircraft. Then I decided – the devil himself gave me the idea – to compete with our Lord Muller. For two years I persisted, spent millions – and lost. Now I'm bankrupt. And I deserve it! I had no choice but to seek shelter in Mullerdom to avoid having to beg. Blessed be Ohisver Muller, our benefactor who takes pity on his enemies and gives them shelter and nutritious cubes!"

"Cut it short, Sir! We're busy here," hissed the man behind the partition impatiently. "Where do you wyyyant to go and how much can you spend?"

"I want wealth. Here, on our benefactor's planet, I wouldn't dare go into anything big. But I saw off a certain publican in West-Wester and saved a decent amount of mulldors, and now I can say I'm ready to start a new life on another planet. I hear that star R25 offers all the right conditions."

"Of course, on R25 you'll become another Muller. The star is young and peaceful; the natives are friendly and entirely defenceless. The going rate to get to R25 is 250 mulldors."

"I don't have that much," wailed the man in tattered clothes.

"Go for a cheaper star then. For instance, 80 mulldors will get you to S6, but don't forget to bring a fur coat!"

"I don't want that!"

"Go to F1 then. A very fertile star, lots of vineyards, grapes with berries the size of your head. Unfortunately, the inhabitants have a strange smell but you'll soon get used to that."

"Why don't you cut the price by five mulldors?"

"Ask the seashell vendor to cut his price. We don't give discounts here!"

Las Abela disappeared and next came a powdered dandy in a white top hat and light grey tail coat. He had a golden jingle bell pinned to his blue tie with a pattern of stars, the latest fashion in Mullerdom. His face was suspiciously young and handsome, but his voice was that of an old man.

"I've had enough of women," he complained, "their bodies disgust me – you can't find anything new any more. The colours change – that's all. I'm looking for new shapes!" His fingers bent like claws and his nostrils quivered lasciviously.

The House of a Thousand Floors

The window smiled kindly.

"Here, have a look at some samples! Of course, not all of them are represented here. Some have bodies that are too different, with unusual forms, made of other substances, driven by different instincts, with different genders. On F9 they inseminate with their mouth, on B11 with a glance, on K12 by touching wings. On X6, they die during intercourse. On U12 they are transparent. On B3 their bodies are as hard as diamond. On H4 they flow, on S22 they burn, and on L7 they're completely invisible. How do you like this female here? She resembles a human being but her blood is cold. These here are the beauties of their species. They have only one breast, sharp as a dagger – you can cover it with a shield, of course – but look at the face! Beautiful – when you get used to it. Intercourse is possible, but no offspring. On T42 they're covered with thick white silky fur. Excellent cooks, they love alcohol, and they prefer to have intercourse with white men – they're terrified of blacks, you see. These, from M14, are really lascivious and understand our boys well. They're slender, like our schoolgirls."

This one, this's the one I want!" the young man gasped with passion. "That's where I'm going first!"

"M14 – 500 mulldors."

"Money is no object! But – when will I get back?"

"In twelve months. You might not even want to come back."

"I'll soon tire of these little girls – and then – the ones with white fur!"

The young man got his ticket and disappeared behind a purple curtain.

A man wearing a black habit with a red rope around his waist pushed his way to the window.

"My name is Richard Alva and I'm going to spread evangelical teachings on other planets," he started in a hollow, ascetic voice.

"You're welcome," came a cold reply, "as long as you have enough to pay with. Missionaries are known for haggling over the price."

"It's a matter of saving innocent beings. An angel of our Lord gave me the idea to depart without delay for L100 in the Chrysanthemum Galaxy. Those poor souls worship an old cracked porcelain pipe the first man threw away there."

"You can't go there. A missionary preaching Islam travelled there last week – and, as you know, having two roosters on one rubbish dump…"

"But think about it!" whined Alva. "Those poor souls will be led astray by a false prophet! They'll believe him and die forever! Let me go there at once before it's too late!"

The missionary leaned into the window, almost overbalancing, and thrust his clasped hands right under the agent's nose. But he got a frosty reply:

"Islam is a faith like any other!"

"But our faith is in danger!"

"All of you missionaries are difficult," the agent sighed. "Do you think they're waiting for you there?" Why do you want to go to L100 of all places? You want to bring the light? Go to C6. It's pitch black there; the natives are blind and worship darkness. They won't be able to see you but they'll hear you perfectly well and you can perform

The House of a Thousand Floors

your miracles as much as you please. I can also recommend E19. The locals are like lambs: they'll believe anything you tell them. You can be their messiah in no time. On K5 Abbé Lar was resurrected and they all agreed to be baptised at once. Frank Farani went to N22 with a circus – and guess what, he became a local god during the opening show. The whole circus troupe make excellent deities, the tent is a temple and the circus show serves as mass. What more do you want?"

The next customer is a landscape painter with a palette and dreamy eyes ready to see the glass bridges and pink waterfalls of W4. After him a smooth barber with a red goatee stiff with brilliantine, like a provocative advertising stunt. He's off to F88 where he'll preach and, with his own hand, spread the culture of combs, brushes, scalp oils and colognes among the hairy locals. A detective with a pipe is heading to K54 on the trail of a murderer. A fading film star wants to rise once more on a new sky and is on her way to cure old age on K7. An heiress is eloping with a penniless poet to L2, the planet of love. A golden-haired beauty is looking for her lover who had disappeared among the stars. A professor of botany with a beautiful sad-eyed wife and a merry knapsack on his shoulder is off to study the flora on F34. A tragic king without a throne is on a mission to find a new kingdom.

One after another, they disappear behind the screen, carrying luggage and clutching colourful tickets. They are crossing this last threshold of our world, never to return, these foolish emigrants leaving their native planet...

XVI

*The lady in black · The treacherous necklace
· "Keep your face hidden…" · Brok takes a close look
· "So I will become a princess among dwarfs…"*

The last one to approach the window was a lady dressed in mourning, all in black as if she had been bathing in a starless night. Her face was covered with a heavy veil; she wore black gloves, breasts safe like a pair of ripening kernels in a still soft shell. Shoulders so thin they were almost sharp, a slender vase of hips, and shapely calves in black stockings disappearing in black lace. All this signalled youth, proud and glorious, although not a single ray of light escaped from her body.

She cast one last fearful glance around. She was the last customer. Without a word, she placed her passport on the counter. The agent looked at it, then he lifted his eyes from the photo to her face, grimacing when he encountered the black veil.

"Would you be so kind as to let me see the original?"

"Is it necessary?" she asked in a low voice, hardly opening her mouth. Then she discreetly dropped a heavy pearl necklace on the counter. The agent grabbed it greedily and put on magnifying glasses to examine it thoroughly, pearl by pearl. Suddenly he laughed with two white fangs flashing in the wide gap of his mouth.

"You can keep your face hidden, Princess Tamara! The necklace betrayed you! You're running away from Gedonia!"

"You're lying!" the lady cried in alarm and her voice broke in the middle of the sentence like a fragile tree branch. The man behind the partition pretended not to hear.

"We have a warrant here for your arrest! Your passport is fake, made by Master Worke from Tiger Street!"

The princess stood there, black and motionless like darkness itself. The veil was hiding her facial expression. All that could be heard was a muffled cry. Then she pressed herself to the window, clasped her hands in front of her chest and whispered with urgency:

"Please, I beg you, don't betray me! I'll give you whatever you want. They've been preparing a terrible fate for me down there. Have mercy! Let me travel to L7! What do you want? This is everything I have…"

The princess spilled the contents of her black handbag onto the counter. Among the pile of jewellery and diamonds gleamed her crown in the shape of a star, each point adorned with a large diamond.

"Is that enough?" she whispered, and then, as if she thought it was not, she revealed her face and smiled. It was a purely feminine gesture, to add the most precious jewel to that which she had already offered.

The invisible Brok had the opportunity to see her close up. What a magnificent smile she had! Her large dark blue

The House of a Thousand Floors

eyes, shaded with long lashes, were the colour of a darkening sky. It was not just the colour but also their bold shape, difficult to define, that added to her exceptional exotic beauty. Her mouth, subtly wide, seductive and passionate, opened in a smile like a ripe red pod with a row of porcelain seeds. Maybe it was her youth that made her face so beautiful in its dissonance of proportion, and allowed the wide mouth to be so alluring.

The agent swept the treasures off the counter and gave her a cunning look.

"You can go then, but you won't escape Lord Muller! He'll pursue you from star to star…"

"Give me a ticket to the most distant one. The last one…"

"Our last stop is the Dwarf Stars in nebula ZB. Not bad, the solar system is similar to ours but in a pocket size. There's a sun a million times smaller than ours. And the planets dancing around it are the spitting image of our planet. The people living on ZB1 look just like us but smaller. One of them will fit into your handbag. But they're giants compared to their neighbours on ZB2. There, they are the size of ants. And the inhabitants of ZB3 were discovered in dust under a microscope. Which one will you choose?

"The first one, since I have no choice —"

"You'll find them to be intelligent, obedient little darlings. You'll feel like you're in a fairytale."

"But how will I hide if he follows me there?"

"You may be glad in the end if someone rescues you from the Lilliput Star. You're bound to grow tired of playing with them after a while. Here's your ticket."

Jan Weiss

"I will become the princess of dwarfs then," she sighed and disappeared behind the screen.

Brok followed her, close on her heels, full of curiosity which tickled his nostrils.

XVII

*The waiting room at the gate to the universe · A pointless debate
· "...the land of our Lord is everywhere..." · The velvet hall
· Brok wants to rescue the princess*

He emerged on the other side looking for an explanation. But he soon understood that between him and the truth stretched a very long white corridor through which he would have to carry the baggage of his curiosity for much longer.

White lamps overflowing with milky light, echoing steps, colliding voices, the emigrants' arms growing longer and longer with the weight of their suitcases, sacks and bags that get heavier with each moment until they begin to graze the floor. After a while, the distance stands still. A long, endless wait. – Then, at last! – Iron gates, solid and heavy, opening slowly and surely like the lid of a coffin. The protesting crowd, exhausted to the point of collapse, rushes through the gaping opening. The last to slip through was the princess followed by Brok. The gates closed behind them softly and irrevocably.

A desolate empty hall was filled with people. As if on cue, they all sat down on their luggage.

"I imagined it to be somewhat different," said the painter, his eyes darting around the empty walls as if looking for paintings.

"If at least they had benches to sit on," complained the missionary who was afraid to sit on his fragile bag. "I have a monstrance in it, chalices and crosses wrapped in vestments," he explained to the detective. "They might get damaged."

The detective rolled his pipe between his teeth with an expression of incomprehension.

"My word!" he said. "This is supposed to be the waiting room at the gates of the universe? This is what waiting rooms in almshouses look like!"

"This is how things end up when you don't distinguish between gold and wealth. On my travels around the world, I used to sit exclusively in first class, in submarines, on boats and airships. I can afford it," said the young dandy. Then he winced and dusted the sleeve of his light grey tail coat when an old lady brushed against him as she pushed her way across the hall to the other end. "Stop pushing, old hag!"

The tall old lady proudly raised her white head. Her hair, parted in the middle, resembled the silver shards of a flying beetle. On top of her head sat a ridiculous little hat, held in place with a black velvet ribbon tied under her chin.

"I am Countess Kokočínová!" she said self-importantly and looked at the arrogant youth through a gold lorgnette."

"Oh, forgive me, Your Highness, I had no idea…" The young man offered an exaggerated apology and lifted his white top hat with ironic gallantry.

"My age creates a lot of problems...," said the Countess in a conciliatory tone.

"And where is your Highness travelling to?"

"Me? I'm going to L70!"

"My word! – The star of love!"

The old lady tapped him coquettishly with her lorgnette.

"You rascal! The star of youth, not love! I'm going to get my youth back. Is it far?"

"Twenty mullerens... I'm not sure you'll live long enough to get there," the ex-millionaire Las Abela said sarcastically.

"But they told me it only takes three nights," the old lady was concerned.

That's possible, but don't forget that time is different in other galaxies, and the ageing process is different there, too, than under our sun."

"Everywhere is our Lord's land," the missionary chipped in. "If it is his will, you will die in Christ on the Cross. I am carrying him with me," he said and piously glanced at his bag. "I even have the holy oil with me for the last rites. Don't worry at all..."

"And I will perfume you for your coffin," said the barber and squeezed the rubber ball of a perfume flacon in her face. A shower of exotic fragrance reached everyone's dry nostrils.

"Me too, me too," cried the pink doll of a girl, suddenly and passionately wanting to smell nice in the arms of her lover.

At that moment, a face appeared above the resting emigrants. It was pockmarked and bracketed between a sailor's cap and a black T-shirt with yellow half moons. Brok recognized the face at once: this was the drunk who had been singing a lewd song on West-Wester's ring road.

"Get up, people, and follow me!" he shouted and lit a cigarette from a burning torch. The low-cut T-shirt revealed his chest with a colourful tattoo of a fantastic airship travelling among the stars. His arms were covered with somewhat unsuccessful creations depicting some hideous stellar vegetation.

He opened a small door leading into darkness and everyone rushed behind him, pushing and jostling. The narrow corridor lazily swallowed them one by one. Damp and long, it rose and fell, like the gullet of an immeasurable snake-like monster. They marched in file, heads low, elbows touching the damp walls. And somewhere far ahead smoked the sailor's torch.

At last, a bright opening, full of hope. The torch disappeared into an alcove; only its red light flooded the moving bodies. And as soon as the princess, with Brok on her heels, passed through the brightly illuminated opening as the last passenger, a door closed behind them.

They found themselves in a round velvety black hall, lit from above by a burning purple globe. Then – desperate cries, weeping, hands waving over heads.

"We've been tricked! We're all going to die!"

At first, Brok understood nothing. Then he noticed a strange, bittersweet smell that made his head spin. A magical, monstrously beautiful flower with blood-red leaves and a black calyx blossomed in his mind. He held his breath and the flower disappeared. They were all pointing up at some white fog exploding from a metal tube in the wall, then dissolving in the air. Panic was spreading.

The House of a Thousand Floors

Brok's first thought was to save the princess. He leapt to the wall in which he sensed the door that had closed behind them earlier. But the door was gone. Meanwhile, he lost the princess in the mad crush. People were throwing themselves about, shouting, crying, holding their noses and covering their mouths.

The former factory owner is circling around the walls with desperate persistence, like a bear in a cage. Richard Alva, the missionary, overcome with the mystical terror of death, is on his knees in the middle of the hall, beating his head against the tiled floor, shouting a blasphemous prayer full of curses and ridicule directed at his god. The poet and the millionaire's daughter fall into a tight embrace, and, without shame in the face of death, they take each other's bodies for the first and last time, with frenzied courage, so that they can die together at the moment of love.

The painter is dying with tears in his dreamy eyes, the barber pulls at his pompous goatee and the dissipated young man eagerly inhales the deadly fragrance into his lungs with deep breaths.

The gas is becoming dense; they all have to let their breath out in the end, and then – drink death gulp by gulp. People fall over one another, their bodies pile up on the black marble.

At last Brok found his princess in the centre of the round hall. She was about to collapse just as he reached her through the crowd. He opened his arms and softly lowered her onto the marble floor. Her eyes widened with surprise.

"Princess! Princess!" cried Brok, touching her temple with desperate lips. "Hold your breath in, for god's sake!"

But with these words, the last breath of uncontaminated air left his lungs. He got up and had no choice but to drink the lethal scent a second time. His head started spinning, he heard the humming of forests in his ears, and the blood-red flower blossomed in his mind again. – This was the end! The end!

So he had lost his battle with Ohisver Muller even before he could start fighting. He had lost before he had the chance to meet him face-to-face. The humming of the forest is becoming fainter and fainter, the black calyx of the flower is growing larger, it opens up and swallows him… Petr Brok falls. The magnesium globe fades. Darkness… no, not even darkness. – Nothing.

XVIII

*The dream · Old man with a kind smile
· Fates of the emigrants · Lousy material
· "And that road sweeper, too!"*

And yet the dirty yellow lamp flickers on. The three-floor row of bunk beds stretches into darkness. There are grey cocoons glued to the bare boards. They appear to have dried out, their surfaces shrivelled. But something is moving inside them, something rank; it's either hatching or already putrefying. There are more of these grey cocoons. They move from time to time, signalling that life inside them continues, that one night a sad velvety butterfly will emerge, a deathhead hawk moth…

And behold! The little yellow lamp with its moonlight glow suddenly bursts into a magnesium flame. Petr Brok opened his eyes.

What happened?

The dream disappeared.

There is a purple fire burning above him again but the bottom of the velvet cylinder is smooth. The round wall appears to have cracked in one place – there is light coming through a narrow gap and something is moving inside it... Petr Brok climbed through the gap to find himself in a steel chamber with no furniture, with riveted walls. A transparent human skull is suspended from the ceiling, with clusters of rays shooting forth from the eye sockets and nostrils.

In the corner is a crowd of pilgrims, half clad, with their hands bound by thin chains. There are no women among them. Brok wondered at first why none of them spoke. Terrible silence emanated from their broken, bewildered faces. Only when he came closer did he realise that they all had metal gags in their mouths. Two drivers in red held them on a harness, each with a cat-o'-nine-tails in his hand. Apart from them and the sailor, there were two other men, whose eyes Brok could look into at close range. He understood at once that these two would decide the fate of the deceived emigrants.

The first of them was an old man with white hair and small dark glasses, and a surprisingly kind smile. From time to time, he would straighten his stooping body dressed in a uniform with gold epaulettes. Several star-shaped medals, arranged into the form of Cassiopeia, were pinned to the front of his uniform. He sported a naval officer's cap with the words 'Admiral Surehand' and a goatee parted in the middle.

The other man's face could not be more different. Ruddy and primitive, it was the face of a brutal butcher. He was dressed in an elegant black suit, like a gentleman, with small diamonds glittering on his fingers, cuff links and shirtfront. His left eye under the sloping forehead was kept open by a monocle which was intended to add aristocratic glamour to his brutal features.

The House of a Thousand Floors

"How many?" the old man good-naturedly asked the pock-marked sailor.

"Forty-five out of ninety," the sailor reported respectfully. "Fifteen women among them. The rest are already in the furnace —"

"Lousy material!" the man with the monocle spat out. "To hell with them!"

"You're exaggerating, Milord," the old man cajoled him. "We'll certainly find something."

He approached the former millionaire and tapped his chest covered with red hairs.

"See this, Milord! The red-haired ones are resilient and live long. He'll make a good miner!"

"Alright, Admiral," replied milord. "Throw him into the mines!"

The sailor wrote something down in a notebook and the assistants dragged the red-haired man to the other end of the hall.

"We need one for the warehouse," milord remembered and approached the barber who was quivering like a bass string. Milord flicked his nose with his index finger, as if in jest, and commented drily: "Floor 567!"

The sailor took note of this and the barber found himself in the far corner.

The admiral noticed the desperate lover whose arms were outstretched towards the iron door heavy with silence.

"Sir Marko is looking for a young slave," he told him in a voice full of consolation. "You're in luck…"

"733!" hissed milord and they went on.

"They need a sweeper on Esmeralda Kranova Street,"

the agile old man rattled, running around in the crowd. He stopped in front of the ex-monarch. "Can you lift a broom?" he asked compassionately. The chubby ex-king, unable to reply, shook his head, visibly offended.

"This is King Aramis the Twelfth," the sailor informed them, having consulted his notebook.

"Which one?" asked milord, as if he had misheard what time it was. He then made a decision and spat out ominously: "To hell with him!"

"To heaven, to heaven," the old man judiciously assured him. "Only rags are burned, and bones make powder for West-Wester's beauties. But the souls fly up to the stars, hee, hee, hee – " He laughed so hard his little glasses fogged up. As he took them off, he revealed two flashing, venomously green eyes, extremely cruel and evil. Once his eyes were visible, his kind, wrinkled face could be seen for what is was: a mere mask.

"Enough!" decided milord. "The rest are all junk! Trash! Burn them!"

"But we need that road sweeper," wailed the old man and put his spectacles back on. Through them he spotted the powdered young man, whose face was twisted into an inhuman grimace by fear and wailing blocked by a metal gag. The sailor noted the floor number and took the young man to the group huddled across the hall.

XIX

*...and now the girls... · The princess lost and found again
· Muller's gallantry · "... give me your smiles, please..."*

"And now the girls," the old man babbled with a lecherous expression on his face, fastening onto his chest one of the stars which had become unstuck. Milord, too, pulled out his cuffs with diamond cuff links as they walked into the next room. Brok slipped in behind them unnoticed.

Inside, a cluster of women writhed and thrashed about on the floor. Brok had seen them moving with the crowd before, lovers and companions, accompanying and accompanied, as well as solitary pilgrims, proudly and quietly following their dream. Their mouths were free; they were not gagged.

"First of all, the princess," Brok thought as he approached the huddle of crying women. But the princess wasn't among them. She was standing apart, her hands clinging to the wall, dark, proud, waiting without a single tear in her eyes.

Brok felt an irrepressible desire to deal with the two villains and free the deceived emigrants. But his instinct, which he trusted above all, commanded him to wait and postpone revenge until that great moment when everyone's turn would come. He tiptoed to the princess, brought his lips to her temple and whispered without touching her with a single hair.

"Do not fear! I am here with you!"

She turned her surprised face to him and her lips quivered with an as yet unspoken question. Brok said quickly:

"Quiet, don't ask about anything! Don't move! They mustn't suspect anything! I'm here by your side. Don't look for me."

He touched her left hand with his finger and whispered: "This is me! This is how you'll be able to tell I'm near you. Will you allow me, please?"

The princess nodded and smiled imperceptibly.

In the meantime, the old crook with the mask of kindness was trying to stop all the tears, cries and curses showered on his head.

"But ladies, dear ladies! — Why all these tears and lamenting? Your noses don't look their best when you're crying!"

"Give me back my boy, my Janíček!" cried the pink girl who still didn't understand what was going on. "I can't leave without him!"

"We've been kidnapped!" screamed the film star hysterically. "Robbers! Air pirates!"

The millionaire's daughter forgot about her poet and mourned her lost luggage.

"If you don't keep quiet, we'll let you taste our fruit!" threatened the man with the monocle. "Our pears are quite hard, I can assure you!"

The House of a Thousand Floors

"Smile! We need your smiles, ladies!" the old admiral babbled on. "Show us your smile while there's still time!"

But the cries, weeping and lamentations only grew louder. The old countess made the worst noise of all. She cried for help, demanded the police, cursed and threatened: "Rascals! Scoundrels! Don't you dare raise your hand against a helpless aristocrat! Where are your stars? In the sky? So you can blackmail, trick and ruin us! – Pirates! Give me back my suitcase! Thieves, I want my money back!"

"The gallantry of our generous Lord Muller is endless," said the monocle and made a pious bow – but there're limits when you're dealing with such trash! Give me the pear!" he commanded, and before the countess knew what was happening, one of the drivers shoved the steel gag in her mouth. – At once, the remaining women grew silent.

"There, my dear ladies! And now I'll ask for your smiles once again! – Look, Milord, this little girl's not exactly a beauty, but she can't be any older than seventeen."

"Of course," the monocle grimaced. "High time for her to join Don Eremis's cabaret..."

After the pink girl, they chose the millionaire's daughter, the botanist's wife with the sad eyes, then two pale, pretty sisters in short skirts and childlike socks, twins, who were like two peas in a pod. They were holding hands and never stopped calling daddy, not understanding anything. The drivers took them away to the corner. There, hanging from the ceiling, swayed a delightful Turkish-style gazebo, upholstered in velvet, with a circle of purple seats.

XX

The first mention of Achorgen · The purple gazebo is a lift · The old procurer comforts the princess · Madame Veroni

The princess was next. Brok pricked up his ears. The admiral smoothed down his uniform trousers with yellow side stripes and razor sharp creases, and approached her respectfully, feigning astonishment.

"Princess Tamara!" he cried. "What a surprise!" – "Our black diamond, lost and found again! A velvet butterfly that wanted to fly away to the sky... we've been looking for you on every floor!"

"Nobody looked for anyone and nothing was lost!" Milord snapped at him. "Nothing is ever lost in Mullerdom!"

But the old man was already happily wagging his chin under a hollow mouth: "Prince Achorgen, Third Secretary of our benefactor Lord Muller, fell in love with you at first sight... He insists that he must be the first to see you perform the crystal whirl, or perhaps second, in case He Himself chooses to... For our benefactor himself has shown interest in you and the progress you are making in dance. But woe betide you now should you, instead of his grace, taste his wrath!"

Jan Weiss

They brought the princess into the gazebo and Brok followed. The old man made himself comfortable and gave a sign with his raised finger. Iron shutters rolled down the sides and the gazebo began descending as a lamp illuminated its interior.

Inside the enclosed cylinder, Brok couldn't tell how fast they were falling, especially since everything around him remained motionless and the lift descended without the slightest sound or tremor. It seemed that the cylinder was standing still and yet he felt that they were plunging into an abyss. For a moment, the little yellow lamp flickered in his mind, but he drove it away.

The old procurer watched the tearmarked faces around him with great interest. There was still the occasional sniffle, a tear rolling down a cheek, but all mouths were quiet. The despair subsided and was replaced with fatigue, and then something new, a momentary flicker of curiosity. Against all expectations, the admiral was on his best behaviour in the falling bell of the gazebo, and he treated the ladies with utmost respect. He was sitting with his trousers upturned, knees pressed together and hands in his lap, so as to avoid any suggestion that he might be keen to touch the women next to him. But he pushed his cap with the gold lettering back and addressed them jovially:

"You see, dear ladies, nothing's happened to you, and nothing will. You were afraid you wouldn't reach your little planet? – I swear by Almighty Muller that we are now flying to a far more delightful star… the star of dance… dance and love… Madame Veroni will teach both of you in her salon. – She no longer dances herself, being some-

The House of a Thousand Floors

what rotund, but she manages a dance academy with renowned artists from the old world... Rest assured, it wasn't just your pretty faces that made us select you, but your bodies and feet also made a difference in the contest of Sleeping Beauties. I even plucked these two rosebuds," he said and his wrinkles deepened in a smile full of kindness. "I couldn't leave such beautiful symmetry behind. We'll find you a father, sweet orphans – you'll have one and you'll have one – but first of all, you'll be sent to school. Madame Veroni will give you a primer of love. – And you, Princess, will return to Villa Tamara, and I strongly advise you to learn the crystal whirl – without dance, there's no career in Gedonia. And seek reconciliation with Prince Achorgen... Don't you understand that all the women down there desire him, and there are princesses among them, too. He's a great man, the right hand of our ingenious divine Muller. And what a gentleman! He occupies an entire floor in Gedonia, three thousand rooms... and he is a generous patron of Mullerdom's artists. If you please him, he will marry you! And he'll take care of you, although he already keeps fifty others in his water harem..."

The princess was looking at the ceiling and said nothing. Her pride, like a light shining inside of her, was as cold as marble and just as unbreakable. Brok was all ears. The admiral's words fell into his mind like seeds on fertile ground.

The bell-shaped gazebo suddenly stopped, smoothly, without a jolt. The shutters flew up and the light inside it went out. The gazebo stood in the middle of a spacious rose-coloured hall. It seemed to Brok as if the music that had been playing somewhere suddenly faded out. All around, people were eagerly running towards them. The open bell was soon surrounded by a sweltering circle of human bodies. Exquisite faces of women with moist, glittering eyes half covered under heavy eyelashes, lips sharply accentuated with lipstick. The men's faces were also made up to look younger, but what was bizarre about them were the goatees most of them sported: black, blond or red, all parted into two strands. Brok recalled some of the faces he had seen in the Adventurers' City; even the kind, wrinkled face of the old procurer was adorned with this strangely shaped formation of facial hair. Brok began to understand that this style must be the current height of fashion in Mullerdom. But there was no time to think about such trivialities. The admiral was the first to step out of the gazebo, smoothing his trouser legs to make their sharp creases stand out.

"Madame Veroni!" he was shouting. "Madame Veroni!"

A corpulent lady emerged from the crowd, her large bosom overspilling from a gorgeous, long low-cut dress made of green scales. Her erstwhile beauty had disappeared under rolls of fat and her mouth above a multiple chin was higher than the top of the admiral's head.

"I am bringing you new angels," babbled the old man, "but you'll have to give their feet wings. I think I chose them well for you."

Madame Veroni observed the pairs of sad little feet through a gold lorgnette, and her rolls of fat quivered with praise. "Excellent job, Admiral," she said. "I've always been happy with your services. Look at these pink

The House of a Thousand Floors

darlings. They'd make our old planet proud, even on Venus. Come and see me tomorrow. We'll settle your bill."

Then Madame Veroni threw her hands up: "By all the suns! This is our Tamara! Admiral, have you been blinded by stardust?"

The old procurer giggled surreptitiously behind his dark lenses.

"Do you really think that I catch only small fry when I cast my nets?"

"Come, my pet," Madame Veroni said sweetly, turning to the princess. "How pale you are! I'll take you to your little villa. Everything is as you left it. You'll see for yourself. Come, you foolish child!"

The admiral didn't like this: "Why don't you stay with your little angels, Madame? They're tired, too! Give them hot water for a foot bath and leave the princess to me. I'll take her where she needs to go. – Forward, princess!"

"Go," whispered Brok.

A fleeting smile passed across the princess's lips and they walked out of the hall: the princess, the admiral and the detective.

XXI

Elvira Karp Street · Villa Tamara
· Petr Brok decides to follow the admiral
· "I'm leaving you just for a short while…"
· Berta Bretard Street · Anna Dimer Street

A square. – Surrounded by palaces made of glass, it looks like the bottom of a large swimming pool with people in fancy dress rushing about. Fantastic wide boulevards radiate into the distance – theatres, cafés, cinemas, museums, casinos and churches, all made of part transparent, part etched glass. Rows of fountains and crystal sculptures, as if chiselled from water, catch the eye with a gleam, then disappear in space as if they had never existed. And above it all, a dome of azure glass, with a never-setting sun suspended in eternal zenith.

> **Elvira Karp Street**
> Donna Elvira was Muller's fourth love

These words screamed at Brok in red letters against a silver background. Brok committed them to memory.

He had to find his bearings, because if he were to lose his way in Mullerdom… No, he must not lose his way! And he also never lost the princess from his sight. He walked close behind her, synchronising his steps with hers. Then, as he stared at the black-clad stems of her calves, he was suddenly overcome with desire. He imagined them bare, and himself very close, transparent like glass. He imagined his invisble arms outstretched, his hands caressing a sleeping body. He immediately felt disgusted at these thoughts and drove them out of his mind. – He'd promised her his help! Yes, he would touch her but only to show her he was near. That's what he'd promised her!

They passed boulevards, crossings, palaces. Pavements ended and new ones started. Avenues of giant cacti and palm trees, carpets of flowers, glass houses, lakes and villas cooled by the breeze of swaying date palm fronds – it was obvious they were in the zone where wealthy aristocrats lived. Finally, they reached a villa bearing a rainbow sign:

VILLA TAMARA

The old admiral bowed before the princess: "Farewell, you proud sinner! I'm going to see Muller now. Pray to him that he is merciful in his anger! His goodness is eternal…"

He remained at the door while the princess ascended a winding staircase without looking back. She appeared again behind the door, and then dissolved into glass panes that kept multiplying – until she disappeared for good.

The House of a Thousand Floors

What now? Brok thought. Follow her? No! For the moment, she's safe. But this scoundrel's going to visit Muller! Let me stay with him.

Brok tore out a page from his notebook and wrote a message:

> *Princess,*
> *I am leaving you for a while. Do not let anyone in. You must hold out. You will know I am here when I touch you.*
> *Your friend*

He hurried up the staircase and slipped the note into a transparent letter box. Then he set out after the admiral. He caught up with him at the crossing, and it occurred to him that he might never find this street again. What was it called?

Berta Bretard Street

read a silver sign, and below:

> The actress Berta Bretard threw herself from the top of Mullerdom because of her unrequited love for the Great Muller

Muller! Muller everywhere! Do all the streets in this city bear the names of his heavy-hearted lovers? Is this god so petty and conceited? Be that as it may, Brok had to remember these names to be able to find his way back. He turned into

Anna Dimer Street

named after a woman who was burned alive for murdering Queen Gertrude out of jealousy and love for Muller.

This street ended with a palace on crystal columns with a wide staircase full of shiny black top hats. A blood-red sign was burning on its front:

STOCK EXCHANGE

XXII

*The golden ant hill · Chubby god under a canopy
· The crystal mouth of the loudspeaker · Stock exchange technology
· Petr Brok learns something about himself
· "You can call him – a divine socialist…"*

The admiral paused under the staircase. He smoothed the creases of his trousers, quickly counted the stars on his uniform, and then cautiously walked up. Brok followed close on his heels.

They entered a vast glass vestibule. Under a gold chandelier of translucent glass globes, a black crowd swarmed. In the centre, a delicate grand staircase rose up to the circular balustrades. In the corner, under a golden canopy, the figure of a terribly fat, double-chinned god was seated in a scarlet armchair. And here, too, the ceiling was fitted with that convex glass, this time with golden rays painted around it that made it look like a sun. Was this a massive lens through which someone's giant eye was looking down as if through a microscope, observing the swarming of bacilli?

The black silk of tailcoats rustles and whispers as bodies rub against each other. Eyes are alight in the blurred

Jan Weiss

faces above dazzling shirtfronts resembling white doors leading to the mechanism of these black figurines which look as if they can be wound up and made to move by a spring, hidden under the black tails. Right hands shoot out and lock into each other as if attracted by magnets. Their chubby fingers are fitted with heavy gold rings.

They are all moving, heading somewhere, and yet their journeys are aimless. They weave through the narrow gaps between the shoulders of others, run around chaotically, return, and form clusters that fall apart as soon as they come together.

Words explode; laughter drums inside throats; cries whoosh through the air.

Petr Brok had lost his way in this tangle of paths, directions and narrow passages. He had lost his admiral. He had fallen into an ant hill and become an ant himself. Running from place to place, climbing and crawling, he listened, clinging to the black clusters of conferring goatees, catching the words they were shouting.

After a while, when his ear began to discern entire sentences, Petr Brok noticed that announcements were coming out of a crystal loudspeaker placed on a high pedestal in the far corner of the hall. Words, slogans, numbers and strange signs were projected onto a white screen and passed on through the lenses of eyes to screens in the brain, inscribing marks on them.

It was here that Brok could fully imagine who Ohisver Muller was, the entire monstrous enormity of this mysterious man who was everywhere and nowhere. This is where low value currencies of other nations fight an uneven battle with Muller's mulldors. This is where his name is pronounced a thousand times a day by a thousand mouths. – It sounded like desperate howling, like a triumphant scream, like pleading for mercy, like the cracking of bones under a heavy boot. The lens in the ceiling became his eye! The microphone in the wall his ear! The crystal loudspeaker his mouth! His hand could suddenly reach in through the walls and, one day, he himself would appear in the mirror…

Who knows whether he was not already present, posing as an investor or broker, or one of the flunkeys… no-one knows him, no-one knows when to expect him…

Petr Brok started to find his bearings. He watched and listened to the aggressive screaming, to numbers, letters and words coming out of the loudspeaker to be then taken up by the crowd who repeated them and distorted them like an echo:

LOUDSPEAKER
     – I will buy fifty black stocks!
SCREEN
     – Rate: 29, 30, 31, 32.50, 33!
VOICES
     – Hear, hear, Muller needs coal!
SCREEN
     – Rate: 35, 36…
VOICES
     – Solium is disappearing
     The miners are revolting
     You can smell the revolution
     They have demolished staircase R
     They have placed mines in shaft B

Jan Weiss

I bid fifty
Hold out
Screen exchange rate 38, 39

VOICES
— Vítek of Vítkovice's coming out of his hole
His head's not above the surface yet
But when it shows, he'll lose it
I bid forty

LOUDSPEAKER
— Done...

VOICES
— A fly has swallowed an elephant
— Today I'm a millionaire
— Let's wait some more
— He's playing us
— He can't get any richer than this

LOUDSPEAKER
— I'll buy 20,000 pairs of hands

More numbers showing the rates flicker on the screen, but Brok is no longer looking. He's walking around, listening:

— Blacks for two mulldors a piece!
— Muller works with whites!
— I bought yellow ones. They work faster!
— But they wear down faster, too!
— I offer whites at five mulldors a piece, Spanish goods!
— They're dumb and lazy!
— French goods are more delicate. I'll throw them on the market when the franc is higher!

The House of a Thousand Floors

LOUDSPEAKER
    – Done!
    – I'll sell 50 wagons of Okka cubes!

– Goods number 256!
– We don't need that! Old stock!
– The warehouses are bursting at the seams!
– Last week I bought half a wagon, enough for two thousand stomachs for five years!
– Yes, Monsieur, the cubes are cheap but the stomachs are expensive!
– In three months, my factory will turn into a hospital…
– A strange disease – the drying of blood…
– Shhh!
– And what about India, Sirdar, is India thankful? Eh?
– Our Okka saved millions during the famine!
– After all, every machine breaks down sooner or later, but we don't need to manufacture man!
– He's overproduced by nature!
– Today, it's impossible to compete without cubes, Grand Vizier!
– The cube in the stomach is not food; it serves to oil the machine!
– A hungry, fussy, lazy, sexually sensitive machine – is it worth it?
– Between us, Mr Ferenc, not even the Chinese can stomach it, let alone dogs!
– I fed my Patagonians with it for seven years! And lost them all!
– Shhh!

— Your Excellency doesn't know how to oil the machine... 250! To hell with it! Mon Dieu!

— Meine Herren, it will fall even further!

— We're all overloaded with cubes!

— Our good Muller will cut the price — for us beggars!

I'll buy half a kilo of radium!

— Listen! Listen!

— Gentlemen, which of you can sell it to him today?

— And what does he need it for, Monsieur Franck?

— He needs rays, Signore, hee, hee, hee — (whispering) for cancer — shhh!

— For his own use, verstehen Sie?

— Shh!

The Persian Shah's throne is for sale!

— Again?

— No wonder! Who hasn't tried it...?

— Allan Gorr didn't last long...

— People are like a wet rag, Milord: the more you wring it, the less it yields...

— I was in Egypt, Mister, thirty-five days for 15 mulldors... an expensive whim... I wanted to be a king, a good one, and make some money as well. — But I was a bad king, and an even worse businessman... mein Gott...

I will lease floor 564 in Mullerdom

— Ha! How much?

– I'll take it right now!
– For how much?
– 750!
– I need office space.
– I want to set up a finishing school.
– I'm looking for a warehouse.
– From floor 900 and up you can see the Garisankar – can you believe it, gentlemen?
– Why not? That's where the lunatic asylums are, hee, hee, hee!
– Shhh!
– On the top of Mullerdom, there's a huge telescope – When his Majesty looks through it as far as the horizon, he sees Mullerdom and himself on top of it – but from behind – ha, ha, ha, ha...
– Shh!

I will sell star K99 with this year's complete harvest

– Was heisst, with the harvest? – Cucumbers, bananas or tomatoes?
– Go and see for yourself, Herr Serafin, or do you think he'll harvest the produce for you and bring it all the way down?
– I've tasted an apple from K84! There were only two samples; one was eaten by the Great Muller himself, the other by myself. That little extravaganza cost me 300 mulldors! – But words cannot describe the miracle that takes place in your mouth! – A taste that's out of this world, your Sunny Highness.

— I tried fruit from K74, Your Highness. They have a slightly intoxicating effect, like champagne. They contain something like stellar alcohol.

— And who would go to K99? — I buy it and then who do I sell to? — I'll end up eating it all by myself, or what?

— I'd try a poisonous cucumber and die, right, signore?

— Shhh!

— Now, of course, it's fashionable to have your own star! Imagine, Don Ortega y Costa, even La Marquise de la Rochefoucauld has her own star, ha ha ha…

— For us, it's dead capital!

— Who would dare travel there, Herr Apfelbaum?

— My son lives on Z19. He's been there for five years already…

— No-one has returned yet…

— Shhh!

— Only a fool would return from paradise to hell…

— But I'm quite happy in Mullerdom, Baron!

— Our benefactor, our Great Father and Lord…

— Of course, we're all in the hands of our Lord, since He's above us…

— And he will forgive us sinners our transgressions…

1 mulldor – 932.896 Dollars –

— Look, Your Highness, the mulldor has fallen!
— Fallen!
— Today — for the first time!
— Yes, for the first time!
— Do you think…?
— Great Muller forbid!

— What do you know, Your Highness?
— I know nothing... nothing.
— Well, why pretend?
— Between us, Your Highness, are you referring to the events in that dive called Eldorado?
— Do you think so?
— No! — Not at all! — What madness! — Could anything shake Mullerdom?
— Of course not — but...
— But?
— Even Muller Himself knows what happened there! Something quite impossible, something that makes no sense...
— If you can believe blind Orsag...
— They're all saying the same thing!
— I don't understand it!
— Chulkov heard a voice!
— Orsag saw him!
— Who?
— A glass container in the form of a man!
— A being made of porcelain!
— The devil!
— God!
— A phantom!
— Chulkov is an old crook!
— Orsag smokes opium! The man was not made of glass or porcelain but of opium haze!
— And what about the shootout with the Unknown Man?
— Drunken delirium!
— But Orsag was summoned to Muller!
— Shhh!

Jan Weiss

I will sell Mullerdom!

— Listen! Listen!
— Muller's selling Mullerdom!
— Is that possible?
— What's happening?
— You're new here, mister? — He often jokes like this with his servants — they say he's weighing up the world!
— It's certainly far-sighted and generous of him. — You must understand, Sirdar, Muller's not interested in his world; he doesn't value it and is ready to sell everything at the drop of a hat, the whole junkyard! Maybe he'll sell Mullerdom, too, Your Excellency, a miracle!
— He'll sell…
— He'll sell…
— He'll sell…
— But for that to happen, you need two…
— And yet, Your Highness, it's very noble of him…
— Muller is a democrat!
— An altruist!
— You could call him — a divine socialist…

XXIII

*I'll buy it! · Two voices have clashed here!
· Petr Brok introduces himself to Muller
· A meeting in Alice Moore Street*

And while such talk travelled through the hall from ear to ear, the loudspeaker said for the second time:

"I will sell Mullerdom –"
"I'LL BUY IT!!!"

The voice came from somewhere in the centre of the hall and cut through the curtain of secretive whispering, insinuations and touches. It was a stone hurled at the mirror in which the hall was reflected, pensive and compliant.

I'll buy it! Someone's buying Mullerdom! Don't we all know that this is Muller's best joke? – Or is there someone mightier than Muller himself? And what is Mullerdom? – A pillar made of solid gold, reaching from hell to heaven!

It appeared as if even the voice pouring out of the crystal loudspeaker was surprised. It wavered – and stopped short. – A moment of terrible silence froze in space. But then the surprise passed and the voice spoke again. – This time, it sounded very different: hard and cruel. Like the creaking of an instrument designed not to kill but to torture:

"Let the man who is buying Mullerdom show himself!"
"Here I am!"

Petr Brok was at that moment indeed in the centre of the hall. He had climbed onto a large transparent statue of Atlas bearing a golden globe on his shoulders. The statue dissolved under him into nothing and the globe remained suspended in space like a fading sun.

And it was here, on the globe, that Brok made himself comfortable. He could safely send his questions from here and catch the answers. He'd decided to make this daring move; his instinct told him that Ohisver Muller was close, the man who became more and more mysterious as he tried to decipher him, more distant as he tried to get closer to him. Here, I finally found a place where I can speak to him; if it is *Him*, that voice coming out of the crystal throat. Very well! If I can seize his voice, I'll be half way to knowing him. The voice that stands out among millions!

Now I have to find the mouth it comes from. The form in which it grows cold and hard like an iron that brands the bodies of martyrs!

The loudspeaker hissed:

"Who are you?"

Well, well, well! Mr Muller was curious! Was he not omniscient? – Brok himself was not sure who he was, and whenever he thinks about it, his temples are crushed in a vice. And then – it is all somehow connected with the yellow lamps that appear in his dreams. – No! He can't think about it! He must believe the papers he is carrying in his wallet. – That's why he has to roam Mullerdom like a ghost, a man without a body – a voice that must kill to find salvation!

The loudspeaker hissed a second time:

"Who are you?"

And the detective said,

"Petr Brok!"

"Petr Brok?"

the loudspeaker repeated contemptuously.

"And I am Ohisver Muller!"

"Names make no difference!"

The sea of top hats deep down under Brok's feet was taken by a storm. Faces grew pale with astonishment. Who is this Petr Brok to whom the name Ohisver Muller makes no difference? The name of the man who owns the universe? The man with the power of God?

Is this other voice coming out of nowhere more powerful? Is it mocking Muller?

Petr Brok! – Is this the name of a man or of a new god?
One thing is certain: two voices have just clashed here! They are weighing each other up before an imminent duel. Everyone has sensed that. – But which one will win?

"Mr Muller, I want to speak to you!"

"Petr Brok will report to agent number 199!"

"I don't need an agent! I want Muller!"

What are the intentions of the voice that wants to buy Mullerdom?

"First of all, I want to ask just a small question, just for your ears: you are selling your house – why so suddenly?"

"I am the one asking questions here!"

"After me, Mr Muller! I know how your star travel works! I know your terrible secrets! The Universe Company... is it not in fact a crematorium? How many shares do you have in it, Mr Muller?"

Now, surprisingly, another voice spoke, much older and somewhat pensive:

The House of a Thousand Floors

"Well then, Petr Brok, tonight you will come to number 99 Alice Moore Street on the 354th floor."

"And who am I to meet there?"

"Ohisver Muller!"

XXIV

*Ohisver Muller's inner sanctuary · "Ascension" wine
· Petr Brok tries Ohisver Muller's patience again
· Three shots into the carpet*

After Petr Brok announced himself to the omnipotent Muller, he didn't dare climb down among the crowd from the golden globe held by Atlas. He waited until people began to leave the hall and the lights started to fade. Then, suddenly, they all went out at once! – Darkness – endless, black, barbaric darkness buried Petr Brok alive!

Oh, woe! – How was he going to get out of here? How would he find the exit? – How was he going to return to the princess he had left in Berta Bretard Street? He now regretted having left her so recklessly. What if she was in danger right now? What if he never found his way back to her?

Brok lowered himself down from the globe and felt his way forward on the carpet. – His fingers touched a cold surface. A tangible point in space! A wall that would lead him to light! Quickly! Move forward! He followed his hand feeling the smooth marble.

Jan Weiss

Finally! – A small door. Behind it lay a narrow corridor and, at the end, another door. – Brok opened it into the light –

Was this a temple, a variety show, a museum, a café or a collection of curiosities? Who knows! Small round tables were standing on colourful carpets with flower designs, around them deep purple armchairs on casters. – Heads are visible above the backrests; people are smoking and drinking hot crimson drinks from silver chalices. – An avenue of luminescent columns leads to a stage with an altar under a starry blue dome. At least it looked like an altar, judging from the symmetrical electric candles, flowers and palm trees. Above the altar was the image of a chubby man dressed in purple, with a crown on his head and a long beard parted in the middle. He was sitting on a throne holding the globe in one hand like a royal orb, and in the other a sceptre in the shape of the house of a thousand floors. An aureole of gold stars was shining around his head.

It was the same jovial man Brok had seen at the stock exchange. A semicircle of violet letters burned above the image:

To Our God Muller!

Brok was all the more surprised to see a row of smaller altars running along both sides of the temple – was it a temple? – with wax figures of strange patrons and martyrs nodding their heads, clasping hands, moving their lips, rolling their eyes and lifting peculiar instruments, the purpose of which was incomprehensible to him.

The House of a Thousand Floors

A wax lady with a sweet smile and a blonde wig, dressed in white draped attire, stood on one of the altars in a glass display case. Her bosom was rising and falling regularly with her breathing and her head was turning with that lovely but also ridiculous movement of a puppet princess whose body is motionless while only the head turns from side to side. A young girl was kneeling at her feet raising her clasped hands in time with the lady's head. Each turn was accompanied by a movement, up and down.

Petr Brok was dumbfounded. At first he wasn't sure why, but soon he understood. He'd seen something like this before. It was a long time ago… it felt as if he was returning to a familiar place he had visited thousands and thousands of years ago. A row of glass coffins containing the wax figures of some forgotten heroes, slowly breathing with the rhythm of a clockwork mechanism. A corpulent lady dressed in white is lying there, her hands crossed on the mound of her rising and falling chest. Here is the leader of a band of robbers, also breathing, then an assassinated emperor over there, and next to him a notorious murderer…

Where was this? And when?

Brok focused on the memory but he felt a vice crushing his head! Ignoring the pain, he closed his eyes and dug into his memory. And suddenly he saw the yellow lamp hanging from a beam… woodworm-riddled pillars and a grey bunk bed with something moving on it… Away! Away with this spectral image! I am now standing in a temple dedicated to the omnipotent, omnipresent, double-bearded God Muller! There are believers lazily lounging in lilac armchairs, sipping from chalices, waiting for something. There is a pulpit in the shape of a golden lily. Like a huge, monstrous pistil, a paunch in a lilac shirt protrudes over it and, above it, a head with a nine-tiered tiara illuminated from inside with a light bulb. Brok saw the moving mouth in the middle of a podgy, full-moon face. Then he realised that someone was speaking and he had to listen.

The priest was praying:

"O Lord, our ruler and king,
You who are called Ohisver Muller,
Meaning the 'eternal wanderer travelling upwards'
You who have created a wondrous miracle
That will be admired by endless generations of this world
The Mullerdom
A bridge leading to heaven
Our Lord, our King,
Ohisver Muller
You who fills the space of this world
With His presence
Descend with your voice among us
As proof for those
Of little faith…

The high priest cleared his throat and raised his eyes as if expecting a voice to come from heaven. When nothing happened, he continued his prayer:

Your will be done
On earth and among stars

The House of a Thousand Floors

Hear our prayers
Great Muller
You, the one, the eternal!
Hear us humbly begging you
Say a single word
And our souls will be filled
With the wine of joy!

The high priest took a breath and prayed for the third time:

All-seeing and omnipresent
All-hearing Ohisver Muller
Pilgrim travelling upward
God of all gods
Master and king of all stars
From among millions you have chosen this one
To dwell on
You have created our heaven among us
And made our earth
The chosen star
The star of god
Our Lord Ohis Muller
Pilgrim travelling upward
Hear our prayer!"

"I hear!"

A voice came down from inside the dome. The high priest rejoiced in his mysterious ecstasy, bells started ringing, an organ started playing, voices sang. The faithful rose and lifted their chalices high. It was clear that this was part of the daily service.

The high priest continued:

"Our God
Architect of Mullerdom
King of the earth
Master of stars!
All the secrets of the universe
And of human souls
Are no longer mysteries
Before You –
Because You Yourself are the greatest
Mystery of the world
You gaze into the depths of infinity
Smiling
Because You see Yourself
Since infinity is Your mirror
You gaze into the depths of human souls
Crying
Because at the bottom You see
The boulders of our sins
Counting the beating of our treacherous hearts
You who have created,
Mullerdom
A bridge to heaven
Forgive us our sins!"

"I forgive!"

replied the divine voice.

The House of a Thousand Floors

Thereafter followed litanies, long and tiresome, which repeated Muller's name over and over again, with thousands of attributes.

Then the high priest stepped down from the pulpit and moved to the main altar where he insistently worshipped God Muller surrounded by light bulbs, asking for a miracle to be performed at this great moment.

And that was when a voice came from above:

"I made this star the heart of the universe
And descended into a human body for a thousand years,
After which I will leave for another star
To build another Mullerdom
The House of a Thousand Floors
But you who are worshipping me
Drinking quantities of hot
Wine of "Ascension"
The symbol of my human form on this planet
You will all live on stars more beautiful and blissful than this one!
For sinners, blasphemers and enemies
I have prepared fire and suffering in the hell
Of nine worlds
For you, my children,
I will prepare heavenly dwelling places on stars
You will be able to choose
In this life
Therefore, I advise you
Not to regret this earth!
Tarry not and look around the stars
To choose the most blissful heaven…

Jan Weiss

And you of little faith,
The reason why I placed solium
Inside this earth
Why I created a fleet
That now plies the universe
Was to draw the sky close to you
And bring the stars to your feet!
Those who believe in me
Will live forever
On the blissful star
They will themselves select
Amen, amen, I say unto you
Prepare for a long journey
Fear not farewells
Entrust your lives to
UNIVERSE
The heavenly transport company."

"A company of procurers, slave drivers and cremators! Do not believe Muller!"

This is what Petr Brok shouted. – He wanted to provoke this false god again! It was irrelevant to him whether it was Muller himself speaking or one of his agents, but he was incensed by that shameless advertising of UNIVERSE.

The faithful responded with dismay. A lightning of terror struck their bristled brains and travelled down the lightning rod of their nerves. The chalices fell from their hands as they fainted with horror. – And from above came the voice:

"The devil came to tempt god!"

"Not the devil or god – a man came to stand up to a scoundrel, conman and a mass murderer! – The whole Mullerdom is one big lie, a fraud!"

Bang!
A shot!
The bullet brazenly whistled into Brok's ear like a street urchin.
Bang!
A second one! This time it flew under his nose, so close he could smell it, and ended up in the carpet, next to the first one.
Beware!
Someone is shooting from above.
Brok's voice became a target. There, a hand holding a Browning was taking aim from a small window in the blue dome.
Was it Orsag who could see him with his lenses?
Bang!!!
Another shot made a hole in the carpet between the two previous ones. Brok did not wait around for the fourth. He rushed to the exit which became a bottleneck for the panicking crowd. – He jumped up on their shoulders and, stepping on a sea of backs and heads, hurried through the portal and down the staircase. He was the first one to reach the street.

Lo and behold! It was Anna Dimer Street, at the far end of which stood the stock exchange with its glass columns.

He remembered how he had penetrated Muller's inner sanctuary through a dark corridor, and tried in vain to explain this coincidence. Instead of the stock exchange, the end of the street was now blocked with the temple and its flashing advertisement

> **To our God Muller!**

Petr Brok decided to solve this puzzle later and concentrated on a far more pressing problem: the princess! What was happening to the princess? He had so thoughtlessly abandoned her in Villa Tamara; what if she was in danger?

XXV

*Prince Achorgen's face · Muller's eye in the princess's bedroom
· To Gedonia by lift · The yellow lamp again*

When Brok arrived at the princess's villa and started looking inside its rooms through the transparent walls, he found them all hidden behind drawn silk curtains hanging from golden rods, reaching all the way to the floor. – But from one chamber with sky-blue curtains he could hear two clashing voices, a man's and a woman's! – Through a narrow gap in the curtains Brok could see the princess sitting and – opposite her on a Turkish divan – a man's head.

Thanks to his invisibility, Brok managed to sneak into the room, soundlessly open a glass door, slip between the drapes under the eyes of the unknown visitor with far more ease than he had expected. He found himself in a young woman's boudoir.

The face he saw against the blue background of the drapes was remarkable. Its features and proportions made it different from any face he had ever seen before. It was a specimen only nature on another planet could have come up with. It was beautiful in its own way, just as the head of a horse can be beautiful, but next to a human head it was astonishing – conspicuously long and narrow, with a magnificently hooked nose like the beak of a parrot. The deep eyes changed colour from yellow to green and from brown to blue, as if reflecting changes of mood. An aimlessly long, desolate upper lip stretched between the nose and mouth. A goatee with two pointed ends was clearly stuck on. His legs were long and thin, and he was taller than the princess by at least two heads. He was dressed in white silk like a tennis player.

"It's up to you," he said. "Everything can be forgotten. Your escape was foolish but it also brought you Great Muller's respect…"

"And how did he find out about my escape?"

Prince Achorgen grimaced with pity at her naïve question:

"Is he not all-seeing? Did you really think you could escape the Eye of Providence? He saw your escape, and followed your every step just as he is now looking down at us from his heaven…" Achorgen pointed to a round glass lens in the ceiling with hypocritical piety.

"Is that his eye?" the princess was astonished.

"Of course it is! On every floor, in all the rooms, he watches his people, day and night…"

The princess lamented: "But there's a little mirror like that in the ceiling of my bedroom, – What shamelessness!"

"Can an all-seeing god be shameless? Of course, he looks into your bedroom, just as he looks into all the bedrooms in Mullerdom! That's why you need not be shy in front of him; he knows you like a husband, although he has never touched you! But now he longs to touch you! –

The House of a Thousand Floors

You've been graced with his attention! – Come, I will take you to him!"

"Never!" the princess cried and glanced around as if looking to be rescued.

"You are proud!" said Prince Achorgen and his eyes grew darker. "There are few women like that in Mullerdom! And Muller needs women like that! – You will no longer be required to dance! He offers you complete freedom of movement on all the floors! You will taste all the pleasures and delights in the heavenly regions of Gedonia if you promise him one single night!"

"I'd rather die," the princess muttered darkly.

"This is precisely the reply Muller is anticipating! If you threw yourself into his arms, he would despise you! He loves a challenge, rebellion, betrayal, – not only on the part of men but also of women. He will continue seducing you for as long as you resist. After he conquers you, he may at best name a street after you…"

Prince Achorgen placed a small bronze lamp on the table, directly under the convex glass in the ceiling. As he lit it, a flame flared out and a grey-blue membrane covered the glass.

Unexpectedly, the prince then laughed. It was a wild, defiant laughter directed at the ceiling. Green light flashed in his eyes.

"Now, my dear delightful little Tamara, – Ohisver Muller has gone blind and deaf for ten minutes! We can do whatever we like, he can't see us… Don't be afraid of Muller – I am here. Only I can rescue you from his clutches! – See, I will betray my master for a single one of your white royal smiles!"

He wanted to take her hands in his, but the princess recoiled in horror.

The prince became sad.

"No! – Don't be afraid of me! I won't harm you... I only wanted to show you my power! As for your love – I'll have to earn it. Come with me! – I'll show you what Mullerdom looks like behind the scenes. All the mechanisms, miracles and magic of divine invisibility, omnipresence and omniscience! – It's a very complex system and there are only two of us who know all about it – Muller and myself! Will you come with me?"

"Go – I am with you," whispered Brok and lightly stroked her elbow.

The princess surprised him by seizing his hand and squeezing it tightly. Brok withdrew it at once but the monstrous face of Prince Achorgen showed no undue concern.

"Will you come?" he asked almost imploringly.

The princess timidly looked around and then said quietly:

"I will."

As they plummeted in the softly upholstered lift into an abyss, Brok once more felt the peculiar illness on his eyelids. – As soon as he closed his eyes, he saw a completely different world around him. And it looked so terribly real as if it were not a dream at all! The accursed cave inside a hollow skull he had seen in the very first dream kept returning to his mind; the same little yellow lamp... And Muller's all-seeing glass eye turned in this skull into a round hole left by a decayed eyeball.

The House of a Thousand Floors

Then again it becomes a small window in a building opening into a wild white storm... Instead of a thousand floors, there are only three, made of grey boards, with living skeletons lying on them curled up in a foetal position. Their chins are warmed between their knees and their mouths breathe onto their numb chests. But it is only when he closes his eyes that he can see all this. – As soon as he opens them again, he finds himself back in Mullerdom. He is falling next to the princess and opposite the parrot-like face of Prince Achorgen who had betrayed God Muller.

How long have we been flying?

Careful!

Just don't close your eyes.

The dream is following you...

To assure himself that the princess was not a dream, he touched her elbow with his finger and she smiled for him...

We are flying to Gedonia...

XXVI

*Monte Carlo in Gedonia · Prima ballerina
· "I don't believe in your stars…"
· Caesar Marlok, God of the Great Sun
· The princess raises her stakes · "This'll be for the journey!"*

A red hall in the shape of a perfect cone is flooded with lights. On the top of a round table standing in the centre, the figurine of a ballerina made of ivory dances on tiptoe. Brok approaches the table to see a polished inlay of precious metals, stones and wood, representing a map of the world. The ballerina is pirouetting on the tips of her toes made of diamonds. Players bet on colours of states, empires and islands. The winning colour is the one the ballerina's diamond toe rests on when she stops dancing. If she ends up standing on the sea, the winnings go to the owner of the casino. The smaller the space people bet on, the bigger their winnings.

The whirling ballerina dances over countries, seas and islands in circles that become smaller and smaller as she crosses the Urals and pirouettes over Siberia. But then she turns south, across the Gobi desert – and she begins wavering, teetering — until she collapses exhausted at the edges of East India.

"Moon yellow — Singapore! — number 29 wins!"

All eyes rest on a gaunt yellow face.

"The Manchurian Governor ShaRa," they whisper. The winner is expressionless, only his Oriental eyes glitter as he watches the flood of gold coming his way. — And the ballerina is dancing again, the gold jingles, piles of golden mulldors grow and tumble...

Petr Brok is standing at the table and he places his hand on a large heap of gold coins. All this could be mine if I wanted it! — Only now does he appreciate what his hand could do among the mountains of gold. So this is the location of the Liquid Mountains mentioned by the old man upstairs? — One labourer's year of work is worth one mulldor! — What a staggering exchange rate!

"One mulldor — six billion lira!" a mouth is shouting behind the grille of a small window set in an oblique wall.

BUREAU DE CHANGE / CURRENCY EXCHANGE

Brok takes a coin from the nearest pile. One side features the sun, the other — stars!

But who are these people with parted goatees throwing handfuls of gold on the colourful map of the world? This is how you throw grain to chickens!

"Look over there, Princess," Achorgen leans over to his lady companion. "That's the new King of Sicily, Malcolm Brooks Pasha. And next to him, the one-eyed man

The House of a Thousand Floors

with a golden collar, that's Genghis Khan La Marten, leaseholder of the Sahara. — He always wins everywhere, except here he's losing in the ballerina game. The man in purple with a triangle on his chest is Muller's Bishop, Sixtus, a former horse trader. And that black man over there? — That's the boxer Kaymann. He's talking to Admiral D'Artois who's rented the title Emperor of all Waters and Governor of Oceans… The fat man next to him is Esaul DarGust, the seasonal inspector of the African coast. He can afford to lose; he's in charge of Muller's treasures. Behind him is Lord Evers, the secret editor-in-chief of all the newspapers of the old continent. And that pixie with the green goatee? Owner of a shipping company on Mars…"

"I don't believe in your stars!" the princess suddenly cried out so loudly that several astonished goatees turned to look at her.

"For God's sake, be quiet!" Prince Achorgen whispered angrily and squeezed her wrist. Then he went on in a more friendly tone: "If that green-bearded dwarf hears you, that'll be the end of you!"

"Don't they know it's all a fraud?"

"Be quiet! Don't shout! They all know and yet they pretend to believe it!" he said and then he raised his voice, glancing fearfully towards the convex lens in the ceiling: "That is the will of our benefactor!"

At that moment, he was approached by an imposing handsome old white man. His perfectly bald, sweating head reflected the crystal chandelier suspended from the top of the cone-shaped ceiling.

Their right hands clasped each other.

"Praised be Muller, Caesar!" Achorgen exclaimed cordially. "What's new on your sun?"

"Thank you for asking, dear Prince," said the old man and his forehead creased with long wrinkles. "Nothing but worries... I visited a week ago... it is indeed difficult to be a just god! I fully understand the Great Muller when he complains to me about his divine duties..."

"This is Princess Tamara," Achorgen introduced his companion. – "Caesar Marlok, God of the Great Sun A3."

"I've heard about you, Princess. Apparently you travelled as far as ZB1 in the Dwarf Galaxy."

The princess wanted to protest but Achorgen squeezed her wrist once more and quickly said: "Of course, she wanted little dolls to play with, a tiny living human doll to bring back to her room. – She's still a child, Caesar. – And how is the game going for you? Have you been lucky?" he asked to change the subject.

"I bet consistently on the black field of Hindustan," replied the bald skull. "I won once and, with those winnings, I can now lose 468 times. – It's a small country, Prince."

"Do you want to play?" Achorgen asked the princess.

The princess smiled dreamily. "I will," she said. "I'll place my bet on the Kingdom of Moravia where my old father is the ruler. It lies on the shores of the Baltic Sea..."

"I wouldn't recommend that," advised Achorgen. "See how tiny your 'kingdom' looks on the skin of the world? Like a mosquito on the body of a mammoth."

"But I'll bet on it all the same, the kingdom I have lost... perhaps I'm going to win back my lost dream..."

The House of a Thousand Floors

"If you win," Achorgen grimaced, "I'll grant you your kingdom on top of the gold."

"And will I be able to go there?" the princess asked naïvely and clapped her hands.

"Of course," whispered the prince into her little ear. "I'll personally accompany you there on my swallow."

The princess places her bet on a tiny, barely visible red drop no-one had bet on before. The winnings could be enormous.

The ballerina starts pirouetting again, setting out from the Island of Pride which has become the centre of the world. She glides with her diamond toe over countries and seas, followed by fervent eyes. She dashes over the azure of oceans, then balances across the grey field of the Balkans, dances over mountains and rivers towards the north, but no-one sees the hand that guides her movement…

Now a sudden cramp shakes her limbs signalling that her dance will soon be over. – A few more drunken movements and the ballerina falls, touching the red drop on the shore of the Baltic Sea with her diamond toe.

It is Petr Brok's doing.

The princess rakes in an entire mountain of gold followed by incredulous looks.

"That'll pay for the journey!" she exults while Achorgen swaps the gold for a few grains of solium in the Exchange Office. He hides them in a pouch, and leads the princess to the door.

They enter a different hall in the shape of a six-pointed star, the glow of which is multiplied into the distance by countless mirrors. – The table in the centre also has six points and there is another ballerina dancing on it.

Jan Weiss

Brok takes a close look. It is not the map of the world, but a black sky dotted with stars. This is where they play for stars. Brok would like to find out more but there is no time. Prince Achorgen hurries through the hall, dragging the princess behind him.

XXVII

*The bedroom of blissful dreams · Pleasures of the six senses
· Heavenly creatures under a transparent ceiling are concerned...
· The bitten-off finger*

They find themselves in yet another hall, no less remarkable, except that this one serves as a bedroom and a film studio in one.

Sleeping bodies are sprawled on divans covered with astrakhan, unseeing eyes half out of their sockets and dilated pupils growing like ink drops on blotting paper. Above them, whirring cameras with reels of film direct their lenses into the eyes of the sleepers.

"This is the bedroom of blissful dreams," Achorgen announced. "The drugs smuggled here by West-Wester's charlatans have the miraculous capacity to make the pupils of the dreamers reflect the wild, exotic, incredible dreams unfolding in their minds. The company

DREAMFILM

pays these wretches debilitated by half-lethal doses of dream pills. The films are then projected onto the silk screens of Gedonia's cinemas."

Jan Weiss

The prince leaned closer to the princess and said in a protectively familiar tone, "I'll show you the film reflected in the eyes of a drunk who uses exclusively FOKA — you'll be astonished at the magnificent fantasy of love! — I can tell you that the films are in three-dimensional colour, and DREAMFILM uses them to show erotic fantasies on non-existent stars to would-be emigrants."

They found themselves on the threshold of a spacious hall flooded with light so bright that Brok was temporarily blinded. — When he could finally see, he registered several impressions all at once.

First: roses falling from the ceiling. They are not really roses; rose-like snow is falling all around on the colourful barricades and nests made of piled-up rubber cushions of all sizes and hues.

Soon his ears caught a sweet, muted melody, as if walled-in; poignant with its illusion of coming from a distance. This is the song of a violin on the top of a high mountain, the weeping of a cello somewhere at the bottom of an abyss...

Brok raised his hand to catch the rose-like snowflakes sprayed around by a crystal fountain in the centre of the hall. He felt a sweet burning chill; it was the pleasure of fire in the freezing cold and the sensation of ice in the middle of a blaze. Insatiable thirst tortured his tongue, while being quenched at the same time...

The bodies of sleeping men and women are lazily sinking into cushions, strings of pearls and tassels on their hips their only attire. The rose-like snowflakes fall on their parted lips, backs, bellies and limbs. Naked female slaves carry around on their heads golden bowls overflowing with wondrous fruits and delicacies.

The House of a Thousand Floors

The eyes of the sleepers are wide open towards the ceiling. What is there? The ceiling is a transparent floor with naked men and women dancing on it. – Hips swaying and grinding to the rhythm of music, arms reaching out into the air for signs of love and passion, legs parting into splits as if the dancers have no bones in their bodies.

"These are the pleasures of the six senses and their worshippers," Achorgen explained to the princess who covered her eyes with her hands.

"Taste these flakes – it is the snow of love from ANDRADIA star. Just stick out the tip of your tongue – and you'll immediately forgive those worshipping its goddess."

He held the princess's elbow and stretched her hand into the snowstorm blowing out of the fountain. The princess suddenly shivered and raised her face to the rose-like shower. She half closed her eyes and parted her lips. Achorgen smiled triumphantly.

"Look up there, my child! – That's where you were meant to be dancing – your hips were to provide a spectacle for these impotent worshippers! But now you can taste these pleasures yourself, and not only these. I'll show you more intense ones, since we're still only at the threshold of heaven!"

Prince Achorgen put his arm around the princess's waist and gently drew her to him. She did not resist. If Brok were to look into her face at that moment, he would have seen her eyelids trembling with desire, nostrils quivering with passion, mouth opening to catch the rose-like flakes…

But instead, Brok was watching one of the pleasure-seekers in whom he recognised the old admiral with his fake mask of kindness and dark glasses. Chin turned upwards, he was stretching himself hedonistically, sinking in feather-down blankets up to his waist, a silver star festering on his naked chest. Brok was curious to hear what he was talking about with the others, all naked and prone on their backs, eyes lazily staring at the ceiling, from time to time shaking off the dew as snowflakes thawed on their bodies.

"Do you believe in miracles, Admiral?"

"Nonsense!"

"How will you explain what's been happening in Mullerdom lately?"

"Of course, our Great Muller has great enemies! He can only be proud of that…"

"So far, he has destroyed everyone who had dared to stand in his way!"

"But today – the danger comes from elsewhere…"

"Do you mean from above, Signore?"

"So far we can only see delightful things above us…"

"The revolution of delicate legs, the stormy waves of hips…"

"Look, Cardinal, I would recognise those gorgeous legs among millions…!"

"Sula May… I can see she has learned to dance…"

"And that pair of virginal calves…"

"Hee, hee, hee! Have you not kissed them yet?

"Muller is not afraid of the devil himself…"

"No doubt! But if he wants to destroy the devil, he has to be able to *see* him first!"

"Look! That's Anna Marton dancing now! Sun Evolution!"

"The slaves' revolt has come closer by sixty floors."

"A floor every day!"

"Oh, that means they still have two years to reach the sky! Vítek of Vítkovice has gone mad, they say…"

"No! He's been murdered!"

"Poisoned!"

"I heard he aged fifty years overnight!"

"Look, Kaja Warand is dancing the roulette on the map of the world!"

"She cost me sixty thousand! I bet on Syria a hundred times – and lost!"

"But can you tell me, Admiral, who could be so audacious…?"

"You can hear a voice…"

"But where is the body? The body that would shed blood… The body that would plummet to the ground…"

"A man without a body!"

"Nonsense!"

"He is God!"

"He is a sheer force!"

"A voice from beyond the grave!"

"The call of the universe!"

"Hostility of the stars!"

"This is no metaphysics, Sirdar! This danger is worse than all the forces and voices from the stars or from the bowels of the earth – He is simply a man!"

"A man? – Have you gone mad?"

"Not just one, a group of people who have infiltrated us, the honest servants of Great Muller! They move among us and they worship Muller together with us; they carry membership cards of our clubs and have enough gold to penetrate all the secrets of Mullerdom! — Yes, gentlemen, there are traitors amongst us!"

"And what about the fight in Hotel Eldorado? And the showdown at the stock exchange?

"And the scandal in Muller's sanctuary?"

"Shots were fired in Eldorado!"

"And in the cathedral!"

"The secret of UNIVERSE has been betrayed!"

"UNIVERSE stocks have fallen from forty thousand to twenty!"

"I have hundreds of them!"

"If we don't destroy that strange force, it'll destroy us!"

"What are you afraid of? We've got Muller on our side!"

"And he'll fall with us."

"Shhhh!"

"Gentlemen, I know the name of that terrible energy that could annihilate us!"

"What is it?"

"Petr Brok!"

"Of course, that's what it called itself when Great Muller asked at the stock exchange with whom he had the pleasure!"

"And today, the two of them will apparently meet at number 99 Alice Moore Street!"

"Muller and Brok!"

"Number 99 — that's the hall of hollow mirrors!"

"It has an electric floor with a trap door!"

"That's where Werner, the very first leader of the rebellion, went mad…"

"That's where Anders, the defiant editor of *Top Floors,* was lost!"

"And where the traitor Olim never returned from!"

"What if the voice doesn't arrive at number 99? What then?"

"He will!"

"What if he can't find the way?"

"He's everywhere!"

"Does that mean he is omnipresent?"

"Just like God Muller!"

"Then he is a second God!"

"And he's present even under this ceiling – among us!"

"Try calling him! He'll respond, you'll see!"

"No! Better not! Why play with the devil?"

"Muller is above us, what are you afraid of?"

"Dora O'Brien is dancing now, the most beautiful woman in Paris!"

"Cowards! Fools! – I'll call him!"

"Quiet! – By all suns, keep quiet!"

"PETR BROK!"

"Don't!"

"Petr Brok! – If you are among us, show yourself, you old bogeyman!"

"Be quiet! Be quiet!"

"If you can, perform a miracle and then I'll believe in you!"

"Enough!"

"Petr Brok! – I am the banker Salmon and this is my hand! Well, if you are as powerful as you make out – he lifts his hand – bite off my middle finger!"

At that moment, the banker Salmon gave an inhuman scream. The short, sharp pain of a severed nerve – a spurt of blood – and the middle finger, complete with a wide black ring, is lying in a bowl, spraying the white salad of edible hyacinths with red."

Sheer terror changed the colour of the faces of everyone present. White faces turned red, red ones turned blue, and blue ones turned black with dread.

But what did Brok care about the grimaces of that lecherous bunch under the transparent ceiling? – In the mayhem that ensued among the worshippers of goddess Andradia, he saw the princess being carried away in Achorgen's arms in the opposite direction to where everyone else was running.

He rushed after her.

They had just disappeared behind a heavy bead curtain in the corner of the chamber. Brok parted the bead fringe and found a white door.

When he opened it, he could see nothing.

XXVIII

*White darkness · Scent and memories
· Again it ends with the little lamp · "This is my past!"*

A milky-white opalescent fog stands in his way. Brok falters, rubs his eyes and fumbles around him.

Three steps before him, two figures melt into the fog, one white, one black: Achorgen and the princess. Brok stepped into the fog with his arms outstretched – but all he could touch was emptiness. The white darkness blinded him. The opalescent silence deafened him.

He ran in the direction where the princess had disappeared. He called out and waved his arms like broken wings. The fog began to choke him; it sang a strange song into his ears. No, it was not the fog that sang like this; it was his own blood gurgling though his arteries!

Every step forward filled him with anxiety. His body refused to move towards the traps lurking in the mist. It was terrible. He moved forward slowly, in the same direction, for a long, long time...

Then he stops short. He is afraid to go either forward or back. He is stranded. Mired in the middle of the white darkness, abandoned by people and things, he had dissolved in an interminable fog. He is lost, swallowed by the white darkness that permeates and fills him. He will lie here, dead, for a long time, and one day, when the white nothing melts away, people will come here, trample over his dead body and no-one will see him...

He could go no further. His legs dissolved under him into the heavy fog. He collapsed crying.

And then – he sniffed. A strange scent flashed through his nostrils; a scent so abrupt that he almost fainted. It rose into his brain like alcohol, half sedative, half stimulant; it painted strange landscapes of the world in front of his eyes. – But what is this quiet soothing smell? – A freshly cut meadow on the edge of a forest. The smell rises from small piles of hay towards the sun like smoke from sacrificial altars. I, too, am lying here in the meadow, hay under my head, hay in my hair, my whole body fragrant with drying mountain herbs. – This is thyme, this here is sage and that is chamomile. When I open my eyes, I see fog dense as cream. I am beginning to remember now. – The princess ran away and there's music playing in the centre of the universe... But the scent, where is it coming from and what does it mean? It's an enchanting melody of scents that soothes and lacerates even more acutely than that sad lovemaking between the cello and the violin playing in the distance.

The smell of the forest reaches him, the smell of moss and pine needles, strawberries and resin. Through the lace of ferns, he can see a spring. Forest birds come to drink here, the deer and the poachers...

But now even this scent has dissolved in the white fog. And another smell wafts over from somewhere. Like

The House of a Thousand Floors

a blustery wind that rises and blows into sails. The cold scent of the sea. The smell of salt and fish scales. The scent of a thawing iceberg floating in the ocean. The mysterious aroma of an unknown island being passed by a ship. There are people there because I can smell sweat and smouldering fires. But then even this smell slowly fades away.

Now, an entirely new smell drifts by, a smell that awakens an old, long-forgotten dream. The heat of a kitchen stove, thick steam rising from pots heralding the midday meal. – Suddenly, a door opens abruptly and lets in a draught. Someone's mouth explodes: war! And everything disappears again, irretrievably.

And now – lily of the valley – no, that's not what it is: it's a drop of perfume on the bosom of my beloved. She bends over me and I take in the smell of her hair to discover a new fragrance.

Now there's the smell of the night. Even the moon has a scent, my god – this is a farewell… this is the green scent of the lake – no, these are tears: the tears of my beloved.

The scents rapidly follow one another:

The smell of a breathless locomotive and of soot;

The smell coming out of open carriages: six horses and thirty men…

The murderous atmosphere of dirt, liquor, foul-smelling feet and latrines;

Distance;

Freshly dug up soil;

Gun powder;

Smouldering camp fires;

Blood;

Jan Weiss

The rank smell of refuse, tins, festering wounds, disinfectant, crushed bedbugs, decaying flesh, frostbite wounds blackly rotting under dirty bandages;

The smell of a yellow oil lamp under the ceiling.

Petr Brok starts. This — this is my past! These are the memories I'd lost. Quickly! Quickly! He stretched out his hands.—Nothing! White fog. A black princess.

There is no other past than Mullerdom.

Brok pulls himself together again and starts running.

Then — his outstretched hand touches soft silky fabric. He pulls it aside — and is astonished at what he sees...

XXIX

*About the star Achorgeneterramolistergen
· Princess Tamara prepares for lovemaking with Prince Achorgen
"...our bed is ready" · Petr Brok uses his invisibility again*

Petr Brok was standing in the doorway of a young girl's blue lounge – the princess's chamber. Muller's round eye in the ceiling is once again covered with a bluish membrane. But the lamp underneath had burned out long ago. The princess is sitting on a blue divan. She is no longer black. She is wearing a sky-blue dress the colour of the drapes in her lounge. She is smoking a cigarette, a tall goblet full of wine at her lips which emanate cascades of bold, provocative, trilling laughter. The ember at the tip of her cigarette draws bold arcs in the air. The crystal goblet and her throat become connected vessels.

And the most terrible sight: Prince Achorgen's impossibly long arm is coiled around the princess's fragile hip. And she's laughing! Mindlessly laughing at something, her face tuned up to the ceiling. Achorgen's arm grows longer, stretching around her waist like a reptile smothering its prey. His whispering mouth is touching her hair: "My lovely star, my silver bell – drink some more. This drink is made from the intoxicating iceberg of my native star. Now you know – I come from planet Achorgeneterramolistergen. Remember it well! You must remember it because that's what I want! Or do you doubt what I am saying?

"Oh, not at all...!"

"You do believe in stars then?"

"I believe whatever you say!"

At the bottom of the goblet is the image of my star. You'll see it every time you empty it. Now finish your drink!"

The princess obediently drained her glass and started laughing again.

"Enough of this laughter! Spit out that jingle bell in your throat! – My child, I am going to love you the way we love on the star Achorgeneterramolistergen. I'll teach you a new way of loving, and you can teach me yours..."

The long snake-like arm around the princess's waist slithers upwards across her breasts up to her throat.

"Do you want that?"

"I do!"

"First of all, give me your hand so I can cover it with kisses... you may suffer for me but your love will cure your suffering. My earthly female, do you really love me?"

The princess rests her head affectionately on his shoulder. The long arm constricts her hips tighter and tighter.

"Kiss me, Tamara! Press your lips against mine; this is how you start lovemaking on this star, isn't it?"

The princess put her arms passionately around his neck.

Brok covered his face with his hands and turned away with horror. – Is it possible? Princess Tamara – *his* princess cast under the spell of this Tower of Babel and waiting to be rescued, is now shamelessly kissing a monster with her unsullied virginal lips.

"Look, our bed is ready, my darling!"

The princess gets up and moves…

Of course, he's a prince and what am I? Nothing so far, an invisible nothing! But this is why I infiltrated Mullerdom. This is why I had undergone this metamorphosis, so that I could find her, protect her and rescue her. Didn't I whisper in her ear that I would protect her? She felt my hand on her arm – and her mysterious smiles – were they not a response to my words?

What betrayal! What shamelessness!

The only ray of light in the whole Mullerdom has been extinguished! Ah – but how can I expect her to love me? How could she if she can't see me?

Away, away from here!

One last look to say goodbye to her. With her hands on her hips that resemble an alabaster vase, she's standing in front of the mirror, laughing. My god, can't she see? Her eyes are closed, her lids heavy. She's laughing with her eyes closed. Her mouth is full of laughter but her eyes are – asleep…

And then Petr Brok understood!

Hypnosis!

He saw Achorgen's burning eyes guarding the princess in the mirror.

Brok lost patience. Angrily he went up to Achorgen and planted a blow between the prince's nose and mouth with his fist. It was as if that spot offered itself to him, the most vulnerable and sensitive in that face. The monster collapsed without the slightest sound. Brok tore one of the drapes into pieces and bound Achorgen's hands and legs, gagged him and stuffed his unconscious body under the bed. When he was finished, he turned to the princess, curious to see her expression.

But she saw nothing, heard nothing. She was still under the spell of the eyes that were now hidden. Her fingers quivered in the silky folds as if they were hiding keys that unlock secret gates among white clouds. The princess began to undress. ...Brok wanted to call out, warn her, wake her up — when, all of a sudden —

XXX

Princess Tamara provokes the darkness
· All that's missing here is a stream… · Beware, Petr Brok!
· A hand can only be held by another hand

he saw her eyes, as they opened against the mirror. She could see her own strange awakening there and, with amazement, she observed her own surprised expression in the silver surface. A heavy, forgotten dream swept across her forehead. Confused, she looks around, rubbing her eyes. But when she wants to grasp the dream, it dissolves in the palm of her hand; under the light blue skies, where blankets and pillows beckon her to sleep. Brok anxiously looks on as she undresses slowly and with the confidence of being entirely alone in the room where she and the mirror are the only living things.

What should I do, what should I do? – No, I can't let her know I'm here. It's too late for that! But I'll guard her in her sleep. She's got no idea that the repulsive Achorger is lying gagged under her bed. But what if he manages to free himself?

That's why I have to stay here and keep guard!

He curled up in a corner, took his heart in his hand

and held his breath. But suddenly he was overwhelmed with a vision: a narrow pink ribbon runs through lace like a sweet promise that is being fulfilled under the sleepy camisole. Away, away with such awful thoughts! Oh, but to approach these lips – what happiness that would be, what happiness!

Her hair, lips, nose, eyes – what a strange and beautiful flower blossomed on the stem of her white neck, what exquisite colours and fragrance! – The face is the most beautiful and precious part of a woman's body which seduces and excites with the naked eye! Look, she's smiling and this makes her even more beautiful because the smile reveals a new colour hitherto hidden among the petals: the colour of snow, milk and porcelain!

For a moment, her dainty shoes dangle on the tips of her toes before they fall off. And before Brok knows it, there is a glimmer of knees and calves, as the gossamer stockings slip on the floor like shed snakeskin. The astonished gleaming surface reflects her beauty, her hands that he yearned for and her breasts rising from the white snowdrifts of lace.

Brok watches this magical performance. How she arches her back and stretches with a tired smile in her triumphant solitude. As if the long hours of having to dissemble in front of people had exhausted her, and only now can she finally cast aside the mask of pretence. With delight she allows her face to relax and she becomes herself again!

Now she's standing here only in a camisole and she continues to tempt her solitude. She cups her small breast in her palm, lowers her head and kisses the nipple. "This is a little boy," she says to the mirror with a smile. Then she kisses the other one. "And this is a little girl. Don't worry little boy. Don't worry little girl. I love you both …" Her caressing words flutter like white butterflies and return to her mouth.

"I am a princess… I am not a princess…," her lowered lips whisper. The words bounce off the cold smooth surface and condense into a misty veil. She wipes the mist off and looks at her reflection up close. Two surprised pairs of eyes marvel at themselves as if they are seeing each other for the first time.

Meanwhile, Petr Brok's patience exults and pulls at its harness, love drums in his blood and roars in his innards. But trepidation gags him. How could he make the princess aware of his presence, his desire, his love? – A single word would make this enchanting vision vanish. How could I embrace her? If I touch her for the first time, her body will not even shiver; perhaps only her hand will move to feel the itching skin. What then? She will become alarmed, frightened – then she will scream with terror!

But Petr Brok has a thousand words ready on his tongue with which to shower her, to weave a net around her, beg her until she is convinced. And yet, will not all the words of love be powerless if she doesn't find eyes to drown in, a body made of flesh and blood that she could possess with all her senses?

The princess approaches her bed, pulls away the blanket, caresses the pillow one last time… and then she collapses, overcome with sudden, bittersweet fatigue. She places her white hands under her head. Her eyes rise to the ceiling, but her thoughts are stronger than the golden stars woven into the blue canopy. They pass across her face, blind her eyes, make her forehead billow, extend and shrink again. Her mouth lies on her face like a bloody heart.

Brok tiptoes to the bed like a thief, barely touching the furs. It's clear that something's bound to happen next – but what?

Brok's face moves close above her mouth. She stares at him fixedly with her eyes wide open and yet she can't see him. Slowly but inevitably, the distance between their lips grows shorter. One last moment and his burning lips fall on her half-open, moist mouth.

Surprisingly, the princess's face remains motionless. Only her eyes wake up and focus as if they have returned from a long journey. Her pouting lips resemble a blood-red rose. But now Brok quickly steps back to avoid the arcs of her raised arms. When the danger had passed and her sad hands fall empty into her lap, he dares to make another move. Lips pressed to her throat, he descends the staircase of kisses to the clearing of her breast, touches the little chapel on its peak, then continues down to the mysterious valley in between, darkened with velvety shadows. Only a little stream is missing here, with forget-me-nots... This is how I would like to spend the rest of my life... falling quietly asleep on this velvety pillow...

The princess is lying silent and motionless, as if dazed in glorious stupor; she's afraid to let her breath out, she wants her heart to stop so as not to frighten this strange dream, this miracle and drive it away; she wants it to continue until its conclusion. – She is being visited by a young, strong god. She can feel his lips, his hands wandering all over her body which is boundlessly open, welcoming, responsive. And all these paths, whether you like it or not, lead directly or in a roundabout way to the very centre of life! Yet his hand appears to be afraid of the end of this vertiginous nakedness. As if confused, it keeps losing its way, it approaches and retreats, travels to faraway regions only to come back again.

But the princess also has hands, don't forget that, Petr Brok, and now you're not going to escape them. Here is your hair, your face — we will come back to that later — and here, these are your hands that betray you with every inch of my body! And a hand can only be held by another hand.

XXXI

*Petr Brok is telling lies · ...I don't have a face yet...
· Muller reminds Petr about the 354th floor
· "...I'm waiting for you..."*

Their hands found each other again and so did their lips.

The princess was whispering: "Who are you? Who are you?"

Brok continued to kiss her without replying. "Tell me, are you the god that has been protecting me?"

"God," said Brok like a coward, afraid he might lose his quarry.

"God," the princess repeated, – "But what kind of god?"

"A good one," Brok wrote on her lips, thinking that he had found the right word.

"I know that you are good," the princess put a distance between their lips again. "But are you young?"

"Young," said Brok, who was not sure himself and was to be tested now. This was the moment of truth. But he sensed that he was going to win. He was convinced of it; every vein in his body knew it.

"Young," repeated the princess… "and handsome?"

"That I don't know," Brok admitted.

The princess's fingers ran across his face. First they discovered a nose, then a mouth, eyes… but how can you ascertain youth and beauty? If she were blind, she might have been able to see with her hands, but since her eyes could not see him, her fingers were unable to recreate his image.

"I want to see you! I want you with my eyes!" she insisted. "Show me your face!"

"I don't have a face yet. I came to deal with Muller…"

"Quiet! Quiet!" the princess whispered anxiously and covered his mouth with hers.

"What are you afraid of, Tamara?"

"He – he can hear everything! His eye above us may be covered up but his ears listen through every crack and cranny!"

"Let him listen! – I'm here to protect you, Princess!"

She smiled at a memory: "The first time you came to me was when I was about to lose consciousness because of the black fragrance in the velvet hall. I could see the steam; I could hear it hissing out of a metal pipe. Unbearable purple light illuminated the pleading hands, the masks of mortal terror and the collapsing bodies… When I myself fell, I found myself in someone's arms. Someone held me and carried me to the stars. It was you… The second time was when I was standing by the wall. You said, 'Don't be afraid! Don't ask any questions! – It's me!' – What happened to the rest of the women who had been left behind?"

"There's a large furnace where they burn human limbs and hearts and mouths and eyes down to a small pile of grey ashes that are thrown into the wind from one of the floors of Mullerdom to disperse in space. They say that that's where they also make powder from human bones."

"How foolish I was, wanting to escape to one of the stars..." the princess whispered and the light in her eyes suddenly dimmed. "At first, I thought that you came to me from the Swan Star. This is where I used to get love letters from when I was still with my father in the Kingdom of Moravia... But there is no Swan Star, no Dwarf Galaxy..."

"It's all a fraud! All of Mullerdom is a fraud, from top to bottom; if there is a top at all... It's run by international slave traders and cremators of dead bodies..."

"Then where did you come from?"

And again she touched his face, felt his skin and measured his mouth with hers.

All of a sudden, Petr Brok felt that he himself was a fraud. Here he was, pretending to be a god to win her love! His passion had long subsided and all that remained was gratitude for each kiss.

"I am no god," he confessed at last, "I am a mere human being, a man!"

She stroked his hair. "Isn't a young mortal better than an old god? – Prove your youth to me! Prove it! Your eyes lie at the bottom of deep valleys and above them your brows are like mountain scrub above an abyss. You are hideous! I might die of terror if I could see you!

And yet, and yet! You have a strong square jaw, a solid, broad nose. The bold arc of your forehead! Thick, pliable hair – this is youth, rebellious, long-haired, and reckless!

I want to see you!

Your massive neck excites my blood! Your giant shoulders could smother me and yet I don't feel your weight at all.

Give me your face!

Descend with your body into my pupils!

You are not a man! You have only taken on a human form, for I can feel you embracing me and kissing me with your mouth. But why can't I see you? I know what I will do! I will make a gypsum mask of our face because it is impossible to love like this… impossible!"

"Be patient, Tamara! – Wait, you'll soon be able to see me. Once I fulfil my mission, I'll become a man again. Tonight I have to go to number 99 Alice Moore Street on the 354th floor. But I've lost track of time… there are no nights or days for me. When was it that Muller told me to come today? It seems that a long time has passed since then! Have I perhaps missed the meeting?

Tell me, my little girl, is it day or night?

Is there no other world than Mullerdom?

Tell me – is the real sun still alive? Can the moon still shine above Mullerdom?

Thirty days…

Which floor am I on? How shall I find Muller?

– How will I kill him?"

Then, a voice came from above:

"Petr Brok!

The 354th floor!

Number 99!

I am waiting for you!"

Brok started. He looked up. The "eye of god" in the ceiling was again rid of the cloudy membrane and stared at him maliciously. Of course! There are millions of eyes and ears on all the thousand floors! But his mouth – does even his mouth reach the princess's bedroom? Does he know that I'm here by her bed? Or does his voice sound through the thousand floors of Mullerdom? ...Brok shivered.

"Can you hear, Princess? He's calling me! I think my time has come. You stay here!"

"I'll come with you!"

She leapt out of bed and started dressing with shaking hands.

"No, no, stay here! – Once I've talked to him, I'll come back!"

"You won't ! – He'll kill you! There are a million tricks and traps waiting for you in room 99!"

"I know his tricks by now! The hall of hollow mirrors! And a trap door behind it! – I'll negotiate with him – in the middle of all the hollow mirrors."

"How will you get there? Do you know your way to the 354th floor? – You don't. See, you're helpless without me! What kind of a god are you? ...My invisible stranger! Come on! I'll take you to the lift."

"Lead me, Tamara! Show me the way before it's too late. Keeping one's word is a sign of strength."

They went out holding hands.

XXXII

Doors white and black · Hall of the hollow mirrors
· Electric signals · Filigree of infinity · Blissful vertigo

The glass street ended with a wire mesh wall reaching to the ceiling. A small door in it bore the sign:

CENTRAL LIFT

The princess opened it by pressing the dot over the letter

They stepped into a square cabin with the walls, ceiling and floor upholstered in leather. On one of the walls was a set of numbers with a thousand white buttons.

"These are the floors, each number is one floor. I fled through here when I still believed in stars."

Brok gratefully stroked her hand.

"For me this is a great discovery! At last I will be able to travel through the entire Mullerdom. But, above all, I will be able to keep the word I gave Muller."

He pressed the button marked 354. The lift didn't move; only the silver hand under the glass shot down to number 354.

"We are there," said the princess.

"Now you go back. No-one must find you on this floor!"

They quickly embraced and parted.

"If I don't return…"

"I'll come looking for you!"

The door opened and Petr Brok stepped into a white deserted corridor so straight and long that the walls, ceiling and tiled floor met in the distance at one single point.

There were doors on both sides. Rows of shiny white doors like those found in lunatic asylums or hospitals. Door after door. All pale, all the same size, equally mysterious; standing there in stubborn silence, offering their handles, with no numbers, no signs…

How will I find the right door? Room number 99?

Brok gently tried the first handle.

Locked!

The second one

Locked!

My God, where do they all lead?

What am I going to do with them?

What's hiding behind them?

Rooms leading to more rooms?

What did Muller have in mind when he sent me here,

into this alley of white doors? What purpose did they serve? Who lived behind them? There's no-one behind them, no sound, and the sepulchral corridor runs as far as the eye can see... How long will I need to try all the doors?

Locked... Locked... Locked...

Yes – with every door I become weaker.

Brok followed the line of the corridor – it had to end somewhere! He ran ahead but the point where the walls met would move away from him just as fast. He felt his powerlessness in front of this enemy called *multitude*...

Then he stopped short. A black door! So sudden, it struck him like a blow. A single black door among thousands of white ones! And on it, scribbled with white chalk, number 99.

Nothing else.

Well, he had finally reached his destination.

Destination? A new trap more likely! A snare – and you, like a fool, will step right in, looking for Ohisver Muller, the bait prepared for you – and then – snap!

Yes, I know all this; I know there's a trap door waiting but tasty bait is sometimes stronger than the threat of death if you look at it intently on an empty stomach. But I'm a mouse that can squeeze even through the wires of a trap cage, Mr Muller!

Brok looks around cautiously. There's no-one, not a soul. He gently presses down the handle, the door opens a crack and Brok slips through. He intends to explore this room before he comes face to face with the mysterious Muller.

A greenish hemisphere opens up above him, reaching all the way down to the ground. More than a hemisphere:

it's the inside of a glass balloon pressed to the ground, without a single edge or a single fold.

Is it a mirror?

An enormous hollow mirror, swallowing Brok from all sides? But how could he tell whether it was a mirror? There was nothing it could reflect – except its own empty interior! Brok quickly turned around towards the door and he froze with horror: it had disappeared behind him! Dissolved into a greenish nothingness.

He felt the walls with his hands. They were all in one piece, ceiling, walls and floor merged into one uninterrupted globe! And although Brok couldn't see himself, it was a mirror all the same! – The smooth inside of the globe reflected its own depths into an incredible distance, multiplying them indefinitely.

This deceptive, detailed infinity is enclosed in a single solid circle which continues as the surface of the floor. And even this floor is an enormous green abyss that reflects and repeats the mute distance of a light green dome arching above it.

And the door, the door has disappeared…

But where did the light come from in this enclosed hollow globe? There was no light source – or did the mirrors themselves cast light? Was the light emanating from them?

And what would it look like if… if I were visible?

Brok stands here suddenly overwhelmed with astonishment, somewhere in the centre of an enormous globe… and what an indescribable blissful vertigo, when you don't know whether you are flying or falling, when you are caught in the middle of an emptiness without direction, feeling your own equilibrium as you are drawn into all directions of the world at the same time by forces of attraction and repulsion!

Petr Brok staggered in this vertigo. And as soon as he took a step onto the smooth surface of the mirror, the sharp whistle of an electric alarm sounded from under his foot. – Petr Brok jumped and another alarm sounded as if he had pressed a button on the wall… Brok moves slowly, cautiously, as if walking on treacherous sharp pieces of glass. But in vain! Each step sounds a signal. The entire floor is covered with hidden alarm buttons. Each spot he touches is immediately betrayed by an ear-piercing shriek.

Brok jumps about a little longer but then he understands that it is in vain, that he's caught in a trap, trap number 99, prepared for him by Ohisver Muller, where there's nothing to hold on to, nowhere to hide.

XXXIII

*A million giants... · Crazy chase inside the globe
· The captured nothing · A small window on top of the globe
· "Is he alive?" · What's important to remember...*

And all of a sudden, a small door opens. Not one, but a multitude of doors appear in the globe, densely placed in endless rows. From each door emerges a half-naked giant with a red sash around his waist. They all look alike. A small head on top of a hairy torso, a net thrown over a bare shoulder. A million giants approaching, as if from the depths of the sea.

Brok leaps towards one of the doors followed by a piercing screech of the alarm, but what he finds is a smooth curved surface. Then, all at once, the doors disappear and the giants step into the globe, swirling the nets above their heads. Their movements are monstrously distorted, their faces warped and elongated in endless chains. A million nets reach for him from all sides. A crazy chase breaks out inside the globe. Brok flees, slides, dodges and skips, bumps into walls. And each of his steps is immediately betrayed to an army of hellishly deformed monsters.

But without the illusion of manifold images, it is just a single man dancing in the restricted space with his net. The accursed alarm system under Brok's feet screams: here I am, here I am! And the sound of the alarm guides the giant towards his prey. The net flies above Brok's head and trails closer and closer at his heels. There's no escape! But he's not going to give himself up so easily! A blow aimed at the chest or face, a kick in the belly... but Brok's foot bounces off the giant's body like a ball thrown against a wall.

In the end, Brok is hunted down and collapses in the centre of the globe. The wide net covers him and tightens around him, his legs and hands are tied behind his body, his eyelids close under the pressure of the ropes. Darkness falls on his eyes.

The last thing Brok sees is a small window opening in the ceiling of the globe. A face appears in it, a repulsive yellow face with a red goatee parted in the middle, two black holes between the cheeks instead of a nose and the lower lip black and parched, hanging down, as if putrefying.

"Is he alive?" a voice is heard.

"He's alive," gasps the giant upwards, wiping sweat off his forehead. But these two voices sound as if they are from his old dream. Two men are bending over him dressed in yellow gowns sweetly smelling of disinfectant. One of them touches the small grey pile with his shoe, and then gingerly removes the cloak covering his face.

"He's alive," repeats a disappointed, impatient voice. – Brok forces his eyes open so as to convince someone terribly healthy and powerful that he is not dead yet.

The House of a Thousand Floors

He sees a small yellow light through the veil of rank air. It's suspended somewhere between the heavy beams supporting this dome of death. Two men smelling of frost and good health load something heavy onto a stretcher. Their arms flexed, they start marching in step, one – two – one – two through the aisle between bunk beds. Only their disappearing feet are visible…

It is all so surprising, so incomprehensible and yet so incredibly simple! It's enough to cover your face with the collar of your cloak and everything disappears and ends. Only the collar of the cloak! You have to remember this!

XXXIV

"...afraid of a captured devil!"
· *How Petr Brok appeared under the lenses of blind Orsag*
· *"What shamelessness!"* · *"Is he handsome?"*

When Petr Brok woke up, the first thing he noticed was that he was still wrapped up in the net but the ropes were much looser. The curled-up knot of his body had uncoiled. He was in a dilapidated empty kitchen. A half-collapsed stove was stranded in the corner. White squares on the walls where pictures once used to hang. In another corner, there was a pile of pots and plates.

A crowd of unknown faces surround him. Eyes popping out, nerves thrilled with curiosity. And yet the knees of the closest gawkers are a good three steps away from the edge of the net, a distance negligible enough to show their bravery and considerable enough to satisfy their cowardice.

And the net is quite peculiar. Not limp as you would expect. If you don't catch a fish, you are unlikely to fill a net with thin air! It falls flat, its strings crumple shapelessly in a small pile. — But this net is firmly stretched, enclosing an oval-shaped empty space, a solidly specific nothing. No-one dares to touch this trembling living *nothing*!

"Ah, you brave knights! Scared of a captured devil!"

A young female in a short colourful skirt pushes her way forward.

"Let me get closer! I'm not scared! – I want to touch it with the tip of my little finger!"

"Let her! She's not satisfied with what her eyes can see. Let her touch! Salmon the banker also sacrificed his finger!"

"Who says she'll put her finger right in its maw? Perhaps she'll touch another place at the opposite end, hee, hee, hee!"

"He won't escape the punishing hand of Lord Muller, after all!" says a little old man with a beard, nodding his small worried head.

"The evil god has been caught in a net!"

"What's he going to do with him?"

"Drown him!"

"Hang him!"

"Strangle him!"

"Are you going to give advice to the Almighty?"

It was the giant who had captured Brok who spoke now. His monumental rock-like chest was puffed up with pride. He jealously circled his prey, keeping an eye out, ready to pounce the moment something moved.

Then the colourful crowd parted, opening a corridor leading from the net all the way to the door. Two men came in. The first was a tall elderly gentleman with a handsome smooth face, well-preserved by wealth. His hawk's nose and cruel blue eyes make him look like a general in civilian clothes. All eyes are on him, all mouths are whispering... And behind him – oh, woe! – Blind Orsag with lenses on his temples.

The leader walked through the corridor with assured, triumphant steps until he was standing by the net. Then he kicked it, as if it were a mere bundle of dirty laundry, and asked Orsag:

"What does he look like?"

Brok shivered.

Is it possible that this blind man can see me? – I myself don't know what I look like! Can someone else tell me? My god, how terrified I am of those round lenses burning their way right into my soul! – I'm afraid, afraid to look into them!

And blind Orsag is already turning the serrated circles behind his ears to adjust the sharpness of the lenses. The hairy giant is the first to interrupt the curious silence with a question that had been hanging in the air:

"Well, Orsag, tell us the truth. What is he wearing?"

"He's not wearing anything," says Orsag. "He's naked!"

"Naked!"

"Ooooh!"

The ladies are horrified and their heart-shaped lips turn into ellipses.

"What shamelessness!"

One of the ladies, with a powdered bosom overflowing from her low-cut dress, faints.

Others flee.

And Brok feels a wave of mad joy!

The blind man can't see my clothes! – How lucky, how

lucky! I have my wallet with documents on me! If Orsag saw it, that would be the end of everything!

In the meantime, Orsag approaches Brok and examines him from up close. He says,

"He's white! – His eyes are white, his mouth, his hair – all white! It seems to me even his blood is white!"

Then he opens Brok's mouth like a skilful horse trader and says,

"He's thirty years old!"

The ladies had meanwhile recovered and begun to move closer.

"Is he handsome?" asked a brunette with gypsy eyes and red-painted nipples.

"How can you ask such a question, Miss Laura? He's naked!"

"Why immediately think the worst...?"

"How dare you, Countess?"

"I believe he's hiding his nakedness better than many of us, ladies!"

"But he's wearing no clothes at all!"

"Are you imagining him like that?"

"Fantasising?"

"Chains!" A voice clattered among the sound of jingle bells like a heavy chain dropped on the ground. It was the general speaking to the hairy giant. His order was fulfilled in seconds.

XXXV

Once again it starts with the little lamp
· Petr Brok keeps his word · Night, plans, escape
· The disintegrating kingdom
· There will be no happiness in the world
as long as Mullerdom stands

Petr Brok had been lying half-conscious, his hands and feet tied to a deep darkness. There were no days or nights in this abyss. From time to time, a little yellow light flashed through his mind, shining dimly though rotting attic beams...

This space with grey cocoons is already part of his dreams. Brok suddenly possesses his human body, visible, full of pain, covered with smelly rags.

From time to time, he would wake up from these dreams and thank God for not having a body and for being a mere voice caught in a net.

This abyss without time or space unexpectedly came to an abrupt end. A white light appeared and thus space returned into the four white walls. A voice could be heard under the light:

"My beloved – my beloved, where are you?"

The princess!

And indeed, her hand is still on the light switch, but her eyes are already with him.

She was black like the first time he saw her at the counter of Universe Company.

"Princess!"

The ropes loosened, his body stretched its back, a wild pleasure of extended tendons sang at the back of his knees.

"Come on!"

She took him by the hand and they tiptoed out.

The central lift.

Dark corridors, dead staircases and again halls followed by more halls...

But an electric torch shone in the princess's hand, showing the way with a single ray of light.

"It's night," Brok whispered.

"Yes, it is night, but Muller can bring the day on any time he pleases! He would light up all the sleeping suns above our heads if he knew about our escape. That's why we have to find our way out of Mullerdom as soon as possible!"

"Out of Mullerdom? Do you know the way? Would you be able to escape?"

"Of course, my strange unknown lover! – Are you satisfied with me? While they caught you, a miserable god, in a trap, I was running around looking for you, preparing..."

Brok shook his head:

"It's impossible to get out of Mullerdom! – And if it's possible, why didn't you escape back to your kingdom a long time ago?"

"I couldn't do it on my own. But I've thought of an excellent ploy. I know where Lord Humperlink lives, the one who kidnapped me from my native land. You will pretend to be Muller – or rather, not Muller, just his voice. You'll order Humperlink to take me back where he brought me from. He won't realise anything's amiss. Muller's voice gives orders to all his subjects! None of them have ever seen his face!"

"We'll see! We'll see!"

And the princess continues, carried away by a magical vision:

"There's a port! – Today it's suspended in mid-air like a table, its edge attached to the wall of Mullerdom. Steel swallows converge here when gold blossoms for Muller. But in the darkness I had penetrated, I could see only the dead metal sleep of these winged sailing boats. Among them I found a small blue bird with a seat for two! You and me... We'll fly to my kingdom..."

The last words were themselves ready to take off. They contained distance and its sweet end. – But the voice at her side sounded hunched, low above the ground:

"I can't! I mustn't! You go alone, Princess, I'll stay here – as long as..."

"Then I'll stay, too!" the princess cried out.

"And how will I hide you, how will I protect you from his revenge? – I myself can hide in a ray of light, in his very eye! – But what shall I do with you? How will I hide your eyes from his? Your hands from his clutches?"

"I know best what could be in store for me, my love. How many times I have fled but now I know this will be the last time! He'd let me run away only to catch me again when he got tired of the game... Then he laughed at me through his spies and agents who were waiting at the end of each of my journeys. Today, by your side, I'm not afraid of his monsters! I fear only his suns, waiting to ambush us in the darkness. I know that today is the last time – but without you, what kind of escape would that be? The blue colibri's waiting – come, kidnap me!

My father's crying on his throne, the last king of the dynasty of white beards. He has no-one he could leave his kingdom to. His only daughter had been carried away by a wizard and the first rosehip grew under the tower... The park around the castle has become overgrown. The branches of the plane trees are pressing at the walls and scraping the plaster away. The larch has sunk its teeth into the battlements. The lilac has pushed its way through the windows and ivy has sneaked up the majestic staircase. Heather and thyme are blossoming on the ledges. My bedroom is overrun with wild roses..."

"My poor sad rosehip fairytale! It'll be difficult to bid you farewell but I can't leave Mullerdom... and you can't stay – go home, fly away! Wait! Tell your father with the white beard what a strange groom you have! Tell him I'll come to ask for your hand one day, a day similar to all the previous ones. And even you won't recognise me because you'll be able to – see me! I don't know what will happen to me when I kill Ohisver Muller. Something will become fulfilled, something will end; a terrible light will go out. Something will collapse... This impossible senseless colossus of a thousandfold madness that weighs down on my mind so heavily! Looming above the world like the insane idea of a drunken devil, it throws its black shadow even over your disintegrating native kingdom at the end of the world.

There will be no happiness and peace in the world as long as Muller is alive and Mullerdom stands.

But it will fall!

It will fall on its own the moment He dies!

That's when dawn will break in my mind and the sun will rise again."

The princess is listening, but her lips are silent, swallowed by darkness.

All the chambers they pass through feel alike with their velvety black silence. – There are many strange objects in them, lying unexpectedly and without any particular reason on the tiles, parquet floors and carpets. They lose their names and language in the darkness. They float at the bottom of the chambers, black, rectangular, mocking. They suddenly appear at the end of the beam of light as if on a fishing rod: the grimace of a grotesquely broken edge, a collapsed shape, slimy shapelessness. The foot stumbles, slips and sinks deep. Something has cracked! Something has splashed! Something is sticking! Something has to be avoided from afar...

"What ugly things," whispers Brok.

"They're not things. – This is the end of them, the destruction of things!"

"What things?"

"Traces of debauchery. This is what heaven looks like after the heavenly inhabitants are gone. Let's walk through here as fast as we can so that we don't run into the army of female slaves who'll come to clean these divine stables."

XXXVI

*Aviators Street · Seagull Lord Humperlink
· The sun over Mullerdom · Brok bid the Princess farewell
· The seat next to her remained empty*

They wandered through a labyrinth of narrow streets whose names awoke in the darkness, stretching in the pale light of the princess's beam. Finally, they reached an iron-clad corridor named

Aviators' Street

A steel door with numerous round bolts bore the exotic names of Mullerdom's pilots:

ARON KORKORAN
The Helmsman of the Crying Swan

ACHIL MOBILES
Captain of the Robber

DOUGLAS GULLIVER
The Parachutist

Jan Weiss

> **BLACK WIND**
> Court Aeronaut of the Southern Cross

> **DUKE LUCIEN D'EAU**
> Airplane with a Trap Door

> **REMUS MAJORESCU**
> Acrobat on the Albatross – Faster than Sound

> **LORD HUMPERLINK**
> The Seagull

"We're here," whispered the princess and stopped Brok in front of the last door. It was locked. The key had been taken out from the inside and the keyhole was dark.

They quickly made a plan. The princess walked to the end of the street and switched off her torch. Brok pressed his mouth to the keyhole and called into the darkness:

"Lord Humperlink, Seagull! Waste no time, saddle the Blue Colibri and prepare to take off!"

He put his ear to the keyhole: nothing.
And then his eye: darkness.
Brok raised his voice and repeated the order. This time he could hear a noise behind the door. Then silence again.
Brok called out for the third time.
And lo! The noise turned into the patter of bare feet. Someone cursed in a low voice. And then – a light came on behind the door and could be seen through the keyhole.

The House of a Thousand Floors

A dishevelled man in a nightshirt looks around with a puzzled expression. Suddenly he leaps to the door and opens it. He has a gun in his hand, suspicion in his eyes, and a predatory desire to pierce the mouth that had been calling through the keyhole.

A hollow darkness yawned through the open door. The man stepped across the threshold and suspiciously looked left and right. Brok took advantage of this moment and slipped into his bedroom where he climbed onto the table under the convex glass on the ceiling. When Lord Humperlink returned, Brok called to him and this time his voice came from above:

"Lord Humperlink, Seagull! A black lady is awaiting you at the end of Aviators' Street. She is Princess Tamara whom you had kidnapped on my orders from the Moravian Kingdom. Now I order you to take her back where you brought her from without delay! That is my will!"

Lord Humperlink listened to the order standing to attention, with an expression of reverent fear in his face and with his hands by his sides, fingers splayed.

"At once, my Lord!" he cried obediently and quickly began to dress. He put on a leather outfit and a helmet with two glass-covered openings. He lit up a torch and set out.

The princess had been waiting at the end of the street. She appeared from the darkness exposed by the blood-red light of the torch, leaning against the wall, black and silent.

"Follow me!" beckoned Lord Humperlink's torch.

Brok tiptoed behind them.

They reached a cast iron gate. Lord Humperlink held the torch close to a black ring in the nostrils of a steel lion guarding the gate. In a moment, as soon as the ring was covered with soot, the wings of the gate silently flew open.

Abrupt, joyful daylight chased away the darkness. The enormous dazzling globe of sun swam in the blue waters of the sky – an incredible sight!

Brok was blinded.

The sun!

Real, living, genuine sun!

And here – it is night!

He found himself on a wide platform surrounded on three sides with glass hangars. Lord Humperlink disappeared into one of them.

Brok quickly approached the princess: "Farewell, farewell, farewell!"

Unable to find any other words, he grew silent and planted long kisses on her forehead, her eyes, her hair. He left her mouth, half-opened in expectation, until last. She wanted to say something but her moist burning lips set his blood on fire. He saw her again undressing in front of the mirror, as if facing the surface of a swimming pool into which she was slowly submerging her nakedness.

Now he has her for a brief moment, leaning backwards in his arms, head thrown back, suffering from love, smiling in glorious sadness under the fiery globe of the sun.

"Will you come later? – Will you follow me for sure?"

"I will! – For sure!"

And how will I recognise you? Tell me a word, a single word you'll whisper to me when you come to us?... Quickly, tell me! So that I'll know you…"

The sound of an engine could be heard in front of the hangar. The princess trembles in his arms.

"Well, tell me, my beloved, who are you?"

"Petr Brok!"

The princess stepped back and stared at the emptiness in astonishment.

"Petr Brok? – *You*'re Petr Brok?"

"I am! – Do you know me?"

I have never seen Petr Brok… But I have heard…"

"What did you hear? But hurry! The Seagull is approaching…"

"I know that Petr Brok once had a different name… He was the only son of the King of Andalusia but he ran away and became a robber!"

"A robber?"

"Yes! And what a robber! He would break into bank vaults, open safes with explosives, and the gold he found he would give to the poor. A robber who stole from robbers."

"I don't know… I know nothing. I remember nothing."

The police were after him for five years but they never caught him! Then, when he grew tired of that game, he gave himself up and became a detective. A detective and a prince! Yes, that's – Petr Brok!"

The blue steel colibri sat in the middle of the platform buzzing impatiently. Lord Humperlink waved from inside.

Jan Weiss

"Farewell, Princess!"
"Tell me once more: Petr Brok – is that you?"
"It is!"

The last embrace plays out in front of the astonished Lord Humperlink and the princess climbs into the back of the blue colibri.

The seat next to her remains empty –

XXXVII

*Sirens and alarms · A warrant is issued for Petr Brok's arrest
· Muller's residence · Brok comes close to Muller
· First, one must bathe*

When the princess became nothing more than a black dot on the blue horizon, Brok returned to Mullerdom and quietly closed the gate behind him. He didn't want to leave any clues that could lead their pursuers to this suspended airfield. Then he decided he would take a rest in Lord Humperlink's empty bedroom until dawn broke in Mullerdom.

But when the gate closed behind him, he found himself in complete darkness. How he regretted not having asked the princess to leave him the electric beam she had used to show them the way. — He groped around in the dark — and stopped in shock!

A shrill alarm sounded above his head, like a whistle with two fingers stuck in a mouth. Then sirens, and finally the corridor leapt out of the darkness under the impact of sudden light.

Windows and doors are thrown open and sleepy, goggle-eyed faces appear in them.

"What happened? What's the matter?"

A booming voice comes crashing down from the ceiling in response:

"Petr Brok has escaped!"

"Catch him!"

A horde of half-naked individuals come running in from a side street. Daggers, sticks, revolvers, nets, lassos, gas masks. – The loaf-shaped lamps on the ceiling shed light on their confused faces, where the terror of the pursued mingles with the ecstasy of pursuit.

Brok joined this colourful crowd as if he wanted to take part in his own chase. He was hoping to find out what they knew about his disappearance and where they were headed. – Thank God they had no idea the princess had escaped!

After a long madcap race through the winding streets, they reached a round square under a glass bell. In a circle around it were the administrative buildings on this floor. One of them, a kind of town hall with a small tower, was covered with various decrees and public notices. Among them was an old warning concerning a breakout of the plague on the 489th floor and a decree about the closure of all exits until the last inhabitants died.

Another notice announced mobilisation against the uprising of slaves on the proletarian floors.

The CREMATORIUM Association advertised painless burning of old and diseased tenants on the floor.

The notorious UNIVERSE offered special discounts for immigrants from this floor to Star L9.

The BROTHERHOOD OF LORD MULLER announced an extraordinary service to honour the blessed Baroness Hortense Muller.

But everyone rushed towards a black poster bleeding with red letters. It read:

ARREST WARRANT
To all tenants on the 376th floor!

The invisible devil Petr Brok who had been taunting our Great Lord Ohisver Muller and was captured yesterday in the globe of green mirrors has escaped!

A warrant has been issued for his arrest by the highest order.

As it is expected that he will continue playing his tricks and disturbing the peaceful lives of Mullerdom's inhabitants, all those living on the 376th floor are advised to be vigilant and to closely guard the streets and their abodes, and report any suspicious movements betraying the presence of the invisible provocateur immediately at the town hall in the ninth department.

Anyone who captures the devil alive or dead will be granted a lifelong stay in Gedonia, 100,000 mulldors and 999 new stars.

Signed Dr Van Gross,
Governor of the 376th Floor

The long and meaningless discussions taking place in front of the warrant began to bore Brok. But then the crowd grew quiet and all eyes were on a man who appeared in the entrance of the town hall.

Brok recognised him at once. He was the general in civilian clothes with cruel blue eyes who had kicked him when he had been wrapped up in the net.

The crowd parted. The general pompously descended the staircase with an expression on his thin lips that betrayed disrespect. He was headed somewhere on his own. Brok followed him, consumed with desire for revenge.

They entered the lift and the general pressed the button marked 100! When the hand stopped on this number, the door opened and Brok found himself in a beautiful park. Dense treetops were decorated with grotesque lanterns which illuminated their fantastic shapes resembling green clouds. Brok slowly followed on the general's heels through an alley lined with palm trees, roses, alabaster statues and opal fountains. They passed under a gate made of thousands of colourful fountain streams coming out of two opposite rows of gargoyles.

In the distance, in the middle of a blue lake, a magical island floated. On it, among the fans of palms and massive ferns stood a palace which appeared to be made of sun rays. Above the lake, the nine-coloured arch of a rainbow created a bridge connecting the island with the mainland. When they stepped on it, the bridge played a sweet melody of nine tones like a strange nine-stringed musical instrument.

Unhindered, they arrived in the first waiting room. From there the only door led into a Roman bath where the general had to submit to a cleansing ritual whether he liked it or not. Brok was forced to watch the skin on the general's back, shoulders and calves turn red under the hands of female slaves. Smeared with fragrant balms and hair oils, and dressed in a Roman toga, he was finally admitted into the second waiting room.

There were five of them sitting there, all scrubbed clean, hungry and reeking of fragrant lotions. Awaiting their audience in snow-white togas, they nervously drummed on the floor with their sandals. Some of them trembled with tension. Their mouths repeatedly whispering: Muller – Muller – Muller!

Among them, Brok noticed the moulting old Schwartz who specialised in the production of Sio gas and whom he had met in Hotel Eldorado ages ago.

The general headed straight for the door hidden behind a purple curtain. On it, black embroidered letters read:

AUDIENCE

The general made a scornful face, almost sticking out his tongue at those five candidates who were alternately turning white with envy and red with anger. Then, as he entered the auditorium, Brok shivered...

At last!

At last, that terrible secret was within his reach – one more step and I'll see – what? A human being?

What does the head that had spawned the monstrous Mullerdom look like?

No matter what it looks like, I will face it at last!

XXXVIII

*God Muller's original · Barricades on the 490th floor
· … I will retreat another sixty floors…
· Vítek of Vítkovice is alive! · Old Schwartz and his gas
· At night, when the enemy falls asleep…*

A royal chamber. Against the background of heavy black curtains, a man is seated on a scarlet throne. His obese body is dressed in a perfect black gentleman's suit. His enormous belly rests in his lap. His face, round, smooth, wise and good-natured, ends in a white double beard reminiscent of God from the Old Testament. His blue eyes stare ahead, dead, as if without lids. He would resemble Buddha if it were not for the beard –

It was the original of the statue made of gold that Brok had first seen at the stock exchange. Even the painting in Muller's sanctuary had him as the model.

And then Brok realised that not even this face was alive.

It was a mere cocoon with glass eyes. The body was alive, it was moving and breathing but what did the face under the mask look like? Why was Muller hiding his true appearance? Was it so terrible that no-one could bear to look at it? Brok feels an urge to pull the mask off his face and look at him, no matter what he looks like!

Attention! The mouth on the throne begins to speak. The lips move gently but the words come out sharp and imperious.

"Marshall Grant! What do you think about the disappearance of Petr Brok?"

The Marshall had been crawling from the entrance towards the throne and only when he reached it did he stand up and began speaking in a humble voice:

"O Lord, the guard Aokun was drugged in the middle of the night…"

"I know that!" The mouth thundered, "Guard Aokun is no longer alive! – But who could have dared…?"

"Oh Lord, I assume there must be more than one invisible devil! There can be no other explanation!"

"Except that the guard's laziness could explain what happened!! And you have disgraced yourself by losing the battle on staircase 555, Marshall!"

"Oh Lord!" Grant wailed. "It wasn't my fault! Those scoundrels broke through ten floors and attacked us from behind!"

"A good general secures his back! You ass! How do you see the situation today?"

"They surrounded three front lines. We had to fight our way through. Nevertheless, our losses are minimal: 8,000 dead, 2,000 wounded and 1,500 taken captive. We retreated 60 floors lower. In zone 490 our retreat was blocked by hastily built barricades."

"I saw your pathetic flight and the various kinds of cowardice it displayed. What's their booty?"

The House of a Thousand Floors

"Insignificant, my Lord! The stores had been evacuated in good time during the retreat…"

"You liar!" the voice shouted. "I saw granaries stuffed with grain. I saw barricades of tinned food. I saw refrigerators swollen with meat. I saw cellars flowing with wine. And all that became their booty! – Do you realize, you ass, that in ten days' time I may go hungry? Do you know what hunger tastes like? You'll find out in the dungeon!"

"Oh Lord!" Grant screamed and threw himself at his feet. – "Give me fifty thousand extra men and I swear I'll chase those scoundrels all the way to the roof. I'll take back every grain of wheat, every tin! I have an excellent plan! We'll retreat down 60 floors more so that their army disperses through the entire West-Wester. We'll fill it with wine and spirits. A hundred wild floors full of pubs, bars, prostitutes and thieves – that's going to dent their enthusiasm and dissolve their discipline. Full cellars will destroy them because they're a very thirsty lot – they're running out of water… Prisoners of war are saying they've already tasted their own urine and have been drinking the blood of the dead!"

"You have brilliant ideas when you're in trouble! Don't forget that Vítek of Vítkovice is still alive! None of those West-Wester villains have managed to outsmart him! – But you'll feed yourself on hunger only when the way to the dungeons opens up for you. Until then take care of your paunch and lard up your stomach so you have something to process! And now – out!"

Marshall Grant stepped back devastated, a defeated general. Little old Schwartz appeared in his place. He fell face down and also humbly kissed Muller's left trouser leg.

"What is your wish, your Lordship?" he lisped in a tremulous voice.

"As you know, your Eldorado companions came to grief up there! The hypnotist Mac Doss never came back from his expedition in search of Vítek. Chulkov with his Kawai came out empty-handed and grateful that he was still alive. Mr Perker was captured and forced to use his own poison. And I remembered you, Schwartz, or rather not you but your gas. Of course, I still have Orsag's bacteria but I need him for other things... Above all, you will show me what you can do! Can you manufacture your gas in large quantities?"

"I fill little pocket balloons, sir, each one is enough to age a single person. I'm a loser, my Lord, without means... nobody wants to grow old voluntarily..."

"How many people can you infect if you start producing Sio wholesale?"

"I can turn the entire Mullerdom into an old people's home!" Schwartz lisped.

"I want you to release Sio against an army of slaves on the 490th floor. There are about 20,000 young slaves. How long do you need to produce the required quantity of gas?"

"20,000 men? – 18,000 gallons, 86 mulldors. Time is no problem."

"Tomorrow?"

"Tomorrow!"

"I must warn you that the slaves are in possession of gas masks. They pilfered them from our stores. They used all our equipment. All attempts to gas them have so far failed!"

The House of a Thousand Floors

"Easy! Our army will pretend to retreat down one floor and meanwhile we'll leave behind sacks with gas in the vacated spaces. At night, when the enemy falls asleep..."

"Enough, Mr Schwartz! I appoint you General Secretary of Marshall Gabler!" – Away with you!"

The little old man kissed Muller's left trouser leg again and scuttled backwards, hands straight alongside his thighs, his backside towards the curtain, until he melted into it.

The next one was the new Marshall Gabler.

He had a bald pink skull, as if made of glass. At first it seemed to Brok that this glass ball had no face, so perfectly round it was from all sides, with two tiny ears attached to the skin. Only from the front did he notice that the surface of the ball had a kind of puckered blemish. It was a small flat surface, like the palm of a hand, but it gathered all possible protrusions and folds with grotesque symmetry. This blemish on the pink ball was the new Marshall Gabler's face.

"Marshall!" said the voice. "80,000 men are awaiting your orders!"

"Sir!"

"Tomorrow morning, General Secretary Schwartz will report to you."

"Sir!"

"You will head straight to the 490th floor in the lift. The army already set out on the Imperial Staircase last night. They'll arrive by morning. Schwartz will tell you the rest!"

"Sir!"

"Now, get lost!"

XXXIX

*Achorgen again · He blew a white feather off Muller's shoulder
· Orsag to the rescue · The fight collapsed on the floor
· "Catch him!"*

When Marshal Gabler disappeared, none other than Prince Achorgen emerged from the black background of the curtain.

Brok was not the least bit surprised.

He had suspected that Achorgen would manage to free himself and return to his master. Then Muller must already know about the princess's disappearance! Brok was curious to hear the discussion between the motionless Muller and his cunning secretary. He might even take off his mask to have a rest from it! – He surely has nothing to hide in front of Achorgen. But to Brok's amazement, Achorgen silently walked around the throne, climbed the staircase up to Muller, placed his hand that had slipped down back on the arm rest, blew a little white feather off his shoulder and smoothed his beard.

Brok was astonished. – Was there no lard or blood in this stuffed sack? The face – yes, of course, it was made of wax, but the rest of the body was a mere dummy? – It wasn't even this Muller? Why were those fools prostrating before him then?

So where was the real Muller?

What about the voice?

Where was his mouth?

Or was it the real Muller who had had a stroke? Perhaps his whole body is paralysed, and only the lungs and heart were still functioning? ...And his brain? His chops?

Brok leapt up onto the throne to make sure. He placed his hand on the left side of the massive chest. There was no heart there! He lowered his ear to the round smile. – No breath!

One more test: stick a pin into the belly! If he's alive, he'll jump!

Then – eeeeee – the rubber wound whistled.

Mr Muller on his throne began to rapidly lose weight. His body was shrinking, the head fell to one side, the whole good-natured cocoon, complete with its beard, was shrinking. Finally, the human proportions of the figurine crumpled into a pitiful small black pile.

Prince Achorgen observed the rapid disappearance of the false Muller with an expression of gleeful surprise. Then, as if he recovered his presence of mind, he warned: "He's here!"

At that moment, a voice boomed from the ceiling: "Orsag!"

The curtain in the background parted and the blind Orsag appeared from among the black folds. Hands on his temples, his lenses keen like the eyes of a predator. He must have been hiding there for a long time; ready to pounce... It was obvious that someone had been expecting Brok to come here! – Was all this just a trap set up for him?

Brok held his breath. But before he could step aside, he felt sharp burning claws on his throat.

"Help!" roared Orsag and a piercing signal sounded from the ceiling in response. Someone up there shouted:

"Achorgen!"

But the prince made no move. He just observed the life-and-death struggle with surprised, incredulous eyes which kept rapidly changing colour in the middle of cowardly wrinkles.

Brok and Orsag had been wrestling upright but now they tumbled down onto the floor and rolled around on the thick carpet. Brok used all his strength to free his throat from Orsag's clutches but found himself pressed to the ground underneath the blind man's body. In a desperate attempt to free his hands, he had to let the enraged Orsag grab his throat again. Using the last remnants of his strength, Brok pulled his arms from under his opponent's knees and, with one violent movement; he tore the lens mechanisms from his temples. – Something broke inside. Brok's throat was free and Orsag's lifeless body collapsed on top of him.

Brok got up. And not before time! The curtain parted again and this time some fifty heads in shiny helmets popped up against the black velvet background.

Brok shot out through the purple curtain, with voices shouting at his heels:

"Catch him!"

The rainbow bridge again sounded its desperate melody under his feet. One last glimpse of gleaming helmets among the palm trees and the disharmony of the rainbow alarm grew distant.

Brok leapt into the lift and pressed the button marked 490.

XL

*Petr Brok wants to save Vitek's workers from ageing
· "The drink of victory!" · The battle on the staircase
· Old Schwartz on the back of a monster*

Yes! His aim was now to save the 20,000 young revolutionaries from the terrible fate of instant old age! And Muller? He'd catch up with him later! – The 100th floor! – It was enough to press the white button, and the rainbow palace with the voice that resides in it was within reach.

Upwards!

But now the lift mechanism seemed to be broken. Brok could hear grating noises behind the walls. The small indicator hand was madly jumping here and there and the lift began to sway. Brok felt dizzy.

Was this his dream coming back?

In one black delirious moment, the lift turned into a strange stretcher on which Brok was resting – Petr Brok! Two men dressed in white coats were carrying him away, everything around them was as white as snow... and the snow was slowly waning, turning black, until there was only darkness. – Darkness without thoughts, heart or brain.

Jan Weiss

It was perhaps just a moment! – A sharp jolt – and Brok came back to his senses. The door opened... was this the 490th floor?

In front of him is an open space that had been turned into a military camp. On both sides there are long rows of tents, and voices can be heard shouting, laughing and singing. There are soldiers everywhere with transparent helmets tapering upwards into a narrow point. – Their uniforms are black and behind red belts there are daggers, knives and revolvers. Ammunition across their chests weighs them down like heavy black fruit.

Some are asleep, snoring in front of the tents, others are enjoying the "drink of victory" while yet others are playing peculiar games with golden stars that can be assembled into fatal constellations. Their hoarse voices sing the praises of the divine leader Muller's fabulous heroic victories on earth, seas and stars.

Brok walked through several passages and everywhere he was met with the same sight: tents, songs, rosaries of grenades around soldiers' waists, and goblets that were meant to fire the heroism of the black mercenaries.

The main staircase appeared behind a half-collapsed wall. It looked different from the first time he had seen it, when he awoke on the red carpet on one of the floors. The carpet was gone and the stairs were covered with black blood. In the congealing pools were drying lumps of cotton wool and discarded bandages. The walls were marked with bullets. Part of the railing with marble globes had been blown up and the electric lights on the ceilings shattered. Enormous spotlights were flooding the battlefield with light.

The House of a Thousand Floors

The broad painful bands of light revealed a high barricade. It was in fact a precariously stacked pile of sacks, barrels and broken wooden crates. Everyone seemed to be busy around a chunky, clumsy-looking machine resembling an old-fashioned fire engine. Some of the mercenaries were pumping; others held sacks and balloons to a metal hose. Old Schwartz was sitting on the back of this monster, lisping orders. The filled balloons were being stuffed into crates and barrels.

Brok understood: Schwartz was mass-producing his gas! He would provoke the slaves to attack, then retreat to a lower floor. The slaves would conquer the barricade and then...

Yes, that's why I've come! To warn Vítek of Vítkovice! To stop him before it's too late!

Petr Brok climbed over the barricade and set off up the stairs.

On the next floor loomed the black barricade built by the slaves. It was constructed with cast iron joists, steel plates, granite blocks, sturdy wheels and plinths of some sort of machinery. In many places, the stone and metal fused into rusty lumps. The half-melted wheels and joists pocked with holes suggested that the barricade had been attacked with fire and acid.

But how could this colossal fused structure be penetrated? If fire could not conquer it, how could I do it with nothing but my bare hands? It seemed to reach all the way to the ceiling!

Then Brok noticed a small gate behind a red-hot metal column. He was able to open it and pass under a steel armour plate.

And that was how Brok made his way into the rebels' camp.

A dark space, bleeding with torchlight. — They have no spotlights here, Brok thought ruefully — not one single lamp... but they were preparing for something on the staircase: the torches were moving up and down in energetic arcs and underneath them were suspended the red blotches of faces. The bodies dressed in rags disappeared, swallowed by darkness.

It was not easy for Brok to slip unnoticed through the commotion of bodies and torches. He wanted to speak to Vítek. But where and how could he find him?

At the top of the staircase, the floor continued into the distance beyond the ruins of collapsed walls. Brok's eyes took time to become accustomed to the flickering blood-red light of the torches with clouds of thick smoke and sizzling drops of burning pitch.

XLI

The prophet number 794
· *"…I will then destroy the living Moloch!"* · *The headquarters*
· *Brok introduces himself to Vítek of Vítkovice*
· *"Postpone your attack until tomorrow…"*

On top of a heap of rubble in a desolate open space behind a collapsed wall stood an old man surrounded by the light of flames. — Above his head a hole gaped in the ceiling, as if it had been left there by the devil himself. The old man loomed terribly above the multitude of slaves and he was blind…

Brok shivered. He was surprised to recognise the blind veteran number 794 whom he had found at the end of his long climb up the staircase. In the blood-red light of the torches he looked like the last apostle who had gathered a hunted herd at the bottom of a catacomb.

"I had waited for ten years," he spoke in an excited voice, "until one day… the wall opened up… A mere human could not have come from there! It was him, our long-awaited Redeemer, the Carrier of Light! He came to lead us out of this Hell of a thousand floors!

Woe to Muller — a thousand times woe!

The hour of punishment has come!

Rise against him and overthrow the yoke of slavery!

Because he said: 'I shall bring you back the sun and love and desires and dreams!'

I will lead you out of the captivity of Mullerdom back to your homes!

And he also said: 'Now I shall descend! I shall work for you below so that you can work for me here!'"

A voice called form the crowd:

"If your new god is so powerful, why doesn't he himself destroy Muller so that we can enter Gedonia without bloodshed?"

The old man cried: "You coward! Did he not say: 'The staircases shall be lit by torches and the ceilings of floors shall burst like drums pierced with a dagger!'

There will be bloodshed on a scale never seen before on the stars! The blood of enemies shall rise and flow over the barricades like over weirs, and flood the staircases like a waterfall..."

Then another voice called:

"Muller promises us life after death on the stars. What does your new god promise us beyond the grave?"

The old man raised his finger to the ceiling through which darkness tumbled down the jagged hole.

"He said: can anything worse or anything better befall you than death? Death, good and quiet, dreamless, like the sleep of a blind child?"

Someone from the crowd protested:

"Why should we think about death when we are going to enjoy the pleasures of Gedonia? We'll send the heaven-dwellers with their full stomachs to take our places in slavery. And we will take their places at the feast, enjoying heaven on earth!"

"Woe betide you if you want to make your stomachs into new gods!" shouted the prophet.

"For He said: 'Enter his temples and bedchambers and dining rooms, chase out false prophets and merchants and sybarites, and your hands will be clean!

You shall topple the idols of Moloch and I shall then destroy the living Moloch himself!'"

Many left the prophet's crowd grumbling and joined another one. There another blind man promised the heavenly joys of Gedonia.

Brok remained with the old man along with a handful of the faithful, listening to his excited prophecies with great interest. He marvelled at how the clever old man thought of using an accidental meeting with him to create a new religion in support of Vítek of Vítkovice! — For a moment, he wanted to manifest his presence so that the crowd would believe the blind prophet but then thought better of it.

He was worried that he might lose sight of his mission and he thought it was high time for him to return to the 100th floor and finish what he had started.

Several signs with arrows pointed the way to the leader. Brok climbed up ladders and through openings in ceilings from floor to floor. At last he stood in front of a door bearing the sign:

HEADQUARTERS

Jan Weiss

He slipped inside together with an exhausted messenger who had just returned from somewhere.

At an oak table, surrounded by his generals, Vítek of Vítkovice sat poring over a map of the Mullerdom battlefield. He was a young man with a shock of dishevelled raven-black hair like darkness itself. He had grey eyes, pale, firmly set lips, a large sensitive nose and an energetic chin as if chiselled from granite. He was chain-smoking, his fingers yellow from nicotine.

"Vítek!" the messenger gasped – "the breakthrough was not successful!"

Vítek's expression remained unchanged. He bent over the map, a plan of floor 490, and stuck a little black flag into one of the squares. There were already three...

The messenger gave a breathless account of what had happened:

"In the spot you had just marked, a company of sappers dug their way into sand! The whole space under the floor of that bedroom was filled with sand up to the ceiling. And there were mines hidden in it. One exploded when it was hit by a pickaxe. Two brothers are dead and five injured."

The faces over the map darkened.

"Accursed floor!"

"This is the fourth time!"

"Everywhere there is sand and nothing but sand!"

"Could those scoundrels have filled an entire floor with sand from top to bottom?"

"It seems that we've taught them how to be clever," said Vítek. "They have guards in all the rooms. The moment they hear shots overhead, they call for back-up and fill the space with sand before we manage to break through."

Another messenger arrived. – Vítek's face showed signs of tension.

"Well?"

"Sand," panted the messenger.

Vítek bit his lip so hard it bled. Another black flag joined the others on the map. "We have no choice but to storm the barricade," he said darkly. "Today!"

He pointed with his finger at another map. – It was long, showing a cross-section of the entire Mullerdom from foundations to the roof. Openings in ceilings and the main lines of the staircases were marked with red flags.

The generals bent over the maps started speaking again:

"It will be a difficult task!"

"There are still 98 floors to go to reach Universe!"

"We've only got enough drinking water left for 144 hours!"

"And enough wine for 60 hours!"

"Then we'll have to turn to West-Wester spirits!"

"Dream powders, bliss pills and cocaine!"

"Woe betide us!"

"Only Universe's airships can save us!"

"It's 98 floors, brother!"

"Brutus!" Vítek turned to one of the generals. "This very night you will lead an attack on barricade number 9. The second barriers will not be any stronger since the black mercenaries are preparing an offensive. Get five thousand men ready and wait for my orders!"

Then, all of a sudden, Petr Brok spoke:
"Vítek of Vítkovice!"
They all jumped up and looked at each other in astonishment.

But Brok continued:
"Postpone your attack to another day. – If you carry it out tonight, you'll be responsible for the extermination of your army!"

Vítek was the first one to collect himself. He shouted:
"Whose voice is this?"

And the voice introduced itself:
"I am Petr Brok!"

"Are you the new god prophet 794 has been talking about?"

"I'm not a god! – I've come to warn you not to attack tonight."

"Why?"

"Don't ask! – Listen to me and you'll see for yourself tomorrow!"

"I believe you and I'll listen to you! – The attack will be postponed…"

Brok disappeared, leaving behind him a tent full of astonishment and joy.

XLII

*The sacks will leak from underneath… · The red triangle
· Old Schwartz's boredom · Before I grow old…
· Button number 100*

In all the spaces he passed through, the rebels were getting ready to go to sleep. A single torch lit the main staircase. Brok quickly slipped through the small gate in the metal barricade. He took a few steps and found himself in front of the enemy barricade. Quietly he climbed over it.

Two men were sitting on crates in the golden spotlight. One of them, a youth, was looking through the barricade. The other was smiling with all the wrinkles in his face. – It was old Schwartz. "Tonight I can sleep peacefully," he lisped, nodding his shrivelled head. "If they try something, we'll fire a few times, just for fun. We'll pretend to defend our positions desperately as if we were leaving behind our young. We will, of course, be forced to flee and that's when we'll hide behind the concrete one floor down. In the meantime, they'll run wild here, like lice…"

"And what if they discover the barrels with your gas? … What then?"

"They won't, rest assured, my boy... The barrels are filled with wine and the sacks floating in them will be leaking from underneath... and there are other barrels, completely innocuous. The ones containing gas are marked with a red triangle and there's one in each corner.

When the signal is given..."

"You have set it up well, grandpa. But what if the robots lie down somewhere else, far from your barrels?"

"They won't, you greenhorn, I've thought it through ... I had it all worked out before you were born. They'll settle around the staircase, like us. Vítek won't let them go any further so they don't get carried away in the bars... do you understand?"

"And what if they follow you in the lift?"

"Ah, you little baby... if Vítek had access to the mechanism of the lift, they'd already be riding up and down and having fun in Gedonia, see? You're still wet behind the ears... aaaah!"

He opened his toothless mouth in a round yawn.

Brok didn't waste any time: he grabbed a wad of cotton wool and stuffed it into the black hole of the old man's open mouth. Then he turned to the curious "baby" and, before he knew what was happening, made him – still gaping – keel over with a single blow to the temple.

In the meantime, the old man proved to be surprisingly quick – he wanted to escape but Brok caught his leg, pulled him back, and tied him up with a long piece of string.

"Fear not, grandpa," he whispered into the old man's astonished eyes. "Sio is not going to harm you! Or are you scared you might shrink by another hundred years?"

Then he took care of the youth, secured him with a string and gag, and quietly crept away towards the tents.

The camp was asleep.

Brok then promptly silenced several bored guards. He immediately recognised the barrels marked with red triangles; he could see rubber hoses tied with a string sticking out from underneath. Brok untied them.

As he released the last one, he felt faint. A red triangle bore painfully into his brain. Brok felt he was losing consciousness, but he gathered all his strength to stay awake.

Away! Away! – Before I turn old!

He staggered forward.

Three more steps – the lift!

One more step – before I fall! At last, with the red triangle painfully branding his brain, he leapt into the lift.

Button number 100! 100! 100!

Brok collapsed.

XLIII

*The 100th floor · "You fell for it, Seagull!"
· Above all, find Muller · These were Muller's bodyguards
· His library*

He dreamt he was lying on a cool bed looking up at the ceiling. It was perfectly white, but in the centre of it was a red triangle. It is so bright, so unbearably red and it is bearing down on his brain with dull pain. It is as if the triangle had a hole in it and someone was trying to force his round skull inside. Ah, if it were not for the triangle…! He would feel so good here! The ceiling is sugar white, so much so that you can feel the sweetness on your tongue. A milky light bulb is suspended from it, like a sleepy water lily bud.

Then suddenly – a jolt!

What happened?

Ah, yes! – The 100th floor!

The open door of the lift, the palm grove, the humming rainbow bridge.

Brok was about to cross the bridge but he stopped at the last moment.

It was impossible!

He would be betrayed.

Muller would immediately be able to tell that someone was coming into his residence uninvited. – It wasn't just a bridge – it was the arc of a harp and every guest had to play it with his steps under the windows of Muller's palace!

He had no choice but to wait and time his footsteps to synchronise with those of another visitor.

Brok didn't have to wait long. He heard the crunch of gravel on the footpath and then none other than Lord Humperlink himself emerged amidst the palm trees. It was indeed him, the Seagull! The last person Brok expected to see! What was he doing here? – A painful memory of the princess passed through his mind. – What had become of her?

The lord set out to cross the bridge without hesitating and Brok kept step with him. – The bridge sounded a melancholy melody that still echoed as they stood at the gate of the palace.

The Seagull submitted to all the procedures required before an audience with Muller, hastily but with pleasure, and at last, dressed in the white attire of a Roman patrician, he stood before Mullerdom's idol.

The bloated Ohisver Muller was again sitting in his place, his belly in his lap, a round smile above his mighty double-pointed beard.

"Oh Lord!" Humperlink cried, touching the carpet with his forehead. "I carried out your order!"

"What order?" the voice boomed from inside the figure.

"I took Princess Tamara back to the Kingdom of Moravia!"

Brok gave a sigh of relief.

"Is that what I ordered?" the voice thundered.

"I obeyed your voice, oh Lord!"

The Seagull then briefly recounted how he had been called, how at first he had been suspicious and had come out with a revolver in his hand, and how he had then obeyed after making sure that the VOICE was indeed coming from the ceiling.

"You were tricked!" came the screeching reply. "You swallowed the hook; you are not a seagull but an ass! That was not my voice! You obeyed the voice of the devil! – Go back at once! Bring the entire fleet into action! It will be at your service! – But do not come back without the princess. Away with you!"

Lord Humperlink disappeared and Brok remained alone in the hall. – He knew he had to act quickly because his Princess was in danger...

He had to complete his mission!

First of all, he had to find Muller!

Search the Palace! All the rooms, alcoves and niches, knock on all the walls, floors and ceilings...

Brok tiptoed to the black curtain behind the throne. He pulled it aside only to find a glass wall dividing the royal chamber in the middle. He squeezed into the other half through a small door. How different this was from the royal half with its bright throne!

Surrounded by a wild primitive mess of the mercenary trade, a dozen muscular half-naked men with shaven square Roman faces were lying around, forming an insane tableau. Their transparent death-resistant helmets and shields were strewn among the mats on which they snored.

They were Ohisver Muller's bodyguards!

Petr Brok tiptoed past them and headed down a long narrow corridor up a winding set of steps until he stood in front of another small door!

LIBRARY

Four walls tiled from floor to ceiling with spines of books, some thick, some slim, some massive like the trunk of an old oak, no longer books.

Let's see, this must be Muller's library!

That could only mean that Muller himself couldn't be far away! Brok opened a few books lying on the table.

Hymns and Odes
Celebrating the Immortal Muller

A Book of Prayers
to the Highest God Muller

How Ohisver Muller Conquered the World
Great History

Ohisver Muller's Conquest of the Stars
History of the Universe

Ohisver Muller's
Heaven and Hell

The Thousand Faces of Ohisver Muller

The House of a Thousand Floors

How Mullerdom Was Constructed

A Guide to Mullerdom

Gedonia and Its Pleasures

The Human Loves of Ohisver Muller
How He Loved the World

OHISVER MULLER
GOD AND MAN
PHILOSOPHY

Brok understood that this terrible harvest of books on all shelves dealt with one topic and one topic alone: the cult of this incomprehensible being. – His curiosity intensified, the closer he came to meeting Muller. – What did he look like? – Who was he?

XLIV

On torturing flowers
· Ohisver Muller is playing in the children's room
· The jewellery case · Rubber larvae made of human skin
· The orang-utan again!

Another chamber:
Glass cases containing silver models of strange instruments and tools that Brok is unable to understand. — Were they perhaps sophisticated instruments of torture, constructed and brought together for the purpose of unimaginable torment? It seems to Brok that some of the shapes suggest they are meant for torturing animals, birds and insects, rather than human beings.

On the table stands a blackened lilac bouquet in a container filled with yellow foul-smelling liquid. Next to it is a parchment-bound volume:

ON THE TORTURE OF FLOWERS
By Ohisver Muller

Brok opened the book at a random page:

Jan Weiss

HOW TO TORTURE A ROSE TO DEATH

A Provence Rose (Rosa Centifolia) in full bloom is separated from the shrub by fire. – The flame must be held at the stem until the rose collapses. The stem is then scraped with broken glass all the way up to the blossom and placed in a vase with boiling water. The vase is then slowly filled drop by drop with a strong solution of vitriolic acid dripping through a glass pipette. An aroma meter measures the rapid rise and fall of the rose's fragrance. Using an aromaphone, you will hear the faint wailing of the queen of flowers. Its colour will fade, subsequently it will turn blue and finally its petals will fall off. – The pistil is then cut out…"

Is this what Ohisver Muller's soul looks like? Is this madness or perversion? Look, a white lily in a vase, infected with black spot. A chrysanthemum suffocated by nicotine fumes under a glass bell. A blood-red peony, its pistil pierced with a poisoned needle, is being fed with alcohol!

Such torture of flowers is of course quite an innocuous game, which shows the infantile nature of the cretinous pervert! But these detailed instruments that only hint at their terrible purpose – are they not models for those used in torture chambers where living creatures are tormented?

Fleeing from this chamber of marvels, the astonished Brok found himself on the threshold of – a children's room! What an incredible contrast! A magical corner full of intimacy and childhood dreams! A cot with net sides ... A toy railway, its large circle spread over a cheerful carpet, with a long train and tiny tin railway station. There's even a tunnel, bridge and a railway switch. – Next to it is a box of building blocks; some are scattered around while others form a half-finished church that will be completed after dinner... A red *laterna magica* with glass slides. Several toy rubber stamps and a piece of paper with the same words printed over and over again, each print fainter than the previous one: Ohisver Muller... Ohisver Muller... Ohisver Muller...

Was it possible that this accursed tyrant and inquisitor had a little son? Or had he created a temple to his own childhood to satisfy his sentimentality? – Did he send the train running around the carpet and project the glass slides on the wall?

So, will there be a family room next to the children's room, with a sewing machine and family portraits on the walls, or a bedroom, or a kitchen with a stove and a shelf full of white cups?

The room was red and empty, except for a small round table in the centre, with a crystal bowl filled with clear water on top. Floating inside the bowl was a human heart...

The next room was blue. Again, there was a crystal bowl with water, but this time there were two sky-blue eyes in it.

Nothing surprised Blok any more. He quickly passed through room after room. At one point, he burst into a rank space crawling with purring and crying black cats. There must have been a hundred of them! After this compost heap, he entered a magnificent hall full of treasures.

Purchased, stolen and misplaced crowns that had belonged to emperors and kings, golden sceptres, orbs, monstrances from cathedrals, ceremonial robes from the Vatican, from Buddhist temples and from the rock temple of the Dalai Lama. Exquisite works of old masters, brought here from galleries all around the now bankrupt Europe, are framed by diamonds as big as a goose egg set in gold.

Rods made of platinum, gold, solium and radium.

Tangled heaps of rings, chains and necklaces.

A barrel full of golden watches!

A chest of earrings!

Rows of cases filled with coins from all around the world…

In the middle of the hall was a gaping black hole surrounded by a railing. To gauge its depth, Brok dropped one of the golden rods inside and counted while listening: nothing!

Then he noticed an electric switch on the edge of the abyss. He turned it and the abyss was flooded with light all the way down to the bottom. And now Brok understood: this was the entrance to a gigantic shaft of a thousand floors which formed the foundations of Mullerdom. This entire bricked up space was an incredible treasure trove where Muller had gathered objects looted from all the corners of the globe.

From here Brok entered a dressing room.

A scaffolding of shelves and rows of hanging hooks held a tangle of junk. Generals' uniforms, impeccable suits once worn by stock exchange brokers, monks' frocks and bishops' vestments, striped sailors' shirts, cowboy hats, top hats, flat caps worn by underworld gangsters, beggars' rags full of holes and patches, white sheets of apparitions.

Strangely, all these had been made to fit a small figure with narrow shoulders and short legs. Some coats and jackets had massive padded shoulders; others had padded fronts to create a fake belly. There was even a coat with a false hump.

One corner bristled with walking sticks, tribal rods, ornamental rods decorated with silver, whips, cat-o'-nine-tails, walking sticks with hidden daggers, bishops' staffs and cripples' crutches. Cabinets held pipes, spectacles, false teeth, ears, noses and wigs. Rubber limbs with spring mechanisms –

And – the most terrible sight – a row of stuffed heads with human faces stretched on them! The work of a taxidermist, these faces had been skinned complete with beards and eyebrows! Flexible rubbery larvae, they would create new unmistakeable human features if stretched over a face!

What a multitude of perfect disguises! A face of a long-deceased man reused like a hat! No wonder not even the devil himself knew what Muller looked like! He roamed the floors of Mullerdom as a general, a one-legged cripple, a portly stock broker with a golden chain across his paunch, or a hunchback. But who was he?

Brok stood at the threshold of another room.

In an open rusty cage a sad tree trunk stood, like a skeleton, with a hideous orang-utan swinging from one of the branches.

Brok stepped back. He was convinced the ape saw him, and indeed, as he appeared in the doorway, the orang-utan bared his wide porcelain-like teeth. Brok recovered his courage and slowly walked step by step under the row of sharp white teeth over his head.

Finally, he reached for the handle of the door opposite, soundlessly opened it and, just as slowly, slipped through before closing the door behind him.

XLV

The omniscience machine · This, if you please, is Him! · A skull within reach · The voices of the stock market

Then he looked around.

A massive, swollen, monstrously complex round thing covered the entire opposite wall of the room. The sight of it made Brok shiver. At first glance, this grotesque cluster of trembling spirals, bells, buttons, pipes and phosphorescent clocks merged into some kind of a painfully surprising formation resembling a living organism rather than an inanimate machine, the insides of a universal robot coming to life...

An endless row of keys, like a long piano, round, of unequal length. In their bloodless fragility they bore a resemblance to the manicured fingers of a dead girl. Brok caught a glimpse of a glass organ, made of countless pipes, each bigger than the previous one. The machine was made of a range of peculiar forms, repeated with unbearable consistency a thousand times. A thousand keys, a thousand bells, a thousand lamps, a thousand bulging little eyes, flashing their glass flames like cats' eyes sending mysterious signals.

Jan Weiss

In the middle of this monstrous organism resembling the altar of a terrible god in its symmetry, a white circle gleamed like a huge communion wafer set in a bizarre monstrance. Under the circle was a calyx-shaped loudspeaker cut out of some precious material.

Opposite this horrifying altar, someone is sitting in a deep armchair with his back to Brok who can only see a tuft of red hair like a tiny flame flickering above the headrest.

Brok held his breath.

Was this Muller?

A small, dwarfish figure, seated at the bottom of a lounge chair. – More like a little girl with red hair – not even the head was visible.

Brok quietly went around the chair.

In it he saw a tiny, dry little man with a hideous face, his body wrapped in a green dressing gown. His mouth was bracketed between two ugly lines and repulsive drooping cheeks. The rolled lower lip was blackened and dried to the gum. A red beard, divided into two under his chin, ran down from his mouth reaching his lap.

And his nose! The bold arc of a vulture's beak. The magnificent centripetal line of a snail's shell. An arc suggesting strength and perseverance. An arc of ridicule, hatred, revenge and victory over the world!

Ohisver Muller!

This, if you please, is Him!

This pathetic yellow dwarf, buried alive at the bottom of an armchair as if in a cracked coffin.

Those hairy ears with blackened lobes! – Were these the ears that made everyone in Mullerdom go silent and tremble with fear?

The House of a Thousand Floors

And these two poisonously green, slimy darting little things surrounded with wrinkles? Were they the all-seeing eyes that looked into the thousand floors and hundreds of thousands rooms at the same time?

Was this the skull in which the monstrous dream of heaven and hell on earth was born?... I have it in front of me, within reach, and I could destroy it... crush it underfoot together with its dream — shatter that gigantic nonsense into a thousand pieces!

Suddenly Ohisver Muller wanted to sneeze. His hand approached his nose, covered it. Brok was curious to see what would happen next and, to his astonishment, the nose — that magnificent victorious nose — remained in Muller's hand, and in its place was a flat thing without bone, merely two holes in a small bump stuck in the middle of a face... He recognised it now, it was the face he had seen in the window that had opened above him when he had lost consciousness in the hall of mirrors.

The victorious nose was placed back.

And why were those slimy green eyes that might sink if they didn't hold on to the wrinkles around them looking so intently at the gleaming white circle?

What was it?

A mirror?

Yes, it was a strange mirror! It had its silvery transparent depth, but nothing in this room was reflected in it.

The mirror was *b l a n k*!

A shiny silver distance at the bottom and nothing more...

Then all of a sudden the impenetrable end of the silver distance came closer — grew darker — and Brok could see indistinct swarming as if he were looking into an ant hill with a magnifying glass that was too strong. Then, as if the magnifying glass were placed nearer, the swarming became blacker, its contours more distinct.

And then – Brok almost shouted:

The stock exchange!

Indeed, it was the stock exchange seen from a bird's eye view!

Brok remembered the glass eye inserted into the ceiling...

He could see the stock exchange with the transparent Atlas in the centre and the ant hill of black top hats –

Now the little man in the armchair reached into the machine with his dry fingers. The machine made a screeching sound like a cat in heat in the middle of a summer night. A silence followed and then the chalice in front of the altar spoke.

Brok realized that it was the stock exchange speaking. A chaotic mixture of mysterious whispers, footsteps and excited cries melted into a single fermenting ball with tailcoats, faces and top hats floating on the surface.

But Muller's hand was reaching for the keyboard again. The sound ball fell apart and two clear voices stood out from the tangle of noises.

"Did you buy?"

"I lost."

"Bad times!"

"The mulldor is falling..."

"How much?"

"25!"

"Oh!"

"Shhh!"

And another two voices:
"What now?"
"99!"
"And tomorrow?"
"Kawai!"
"That damned voice!"
"He escaped!"
"He killed Orsag!"
"He tore out his eyes!"
"Who?"
"The voice!"
"And the Great Muller?"
"Shhh!"

And another dialogue:
"The white ones are losing value!"
"The princess has escaped!"
"He abducted her!"
"Who?"
"The voice!"
"And our lord and provider?"
"Enough of this sweet talk!"
"The end is nigh!"
"Shhh!"
"Why be afraid? Something greater than Muller himself is coming!"
"The secret of UNIVERSE revealed!"
"God was unmasked!"
"The stock exchange has crashed!"

Jan Weiss

"Well, who'll come out the winner?"
"Shhh!"
"Stop hissing!"
"Muller will fall!"
"Fall!"
"And who will win…?"
"Him!"
"The voice!"

XLVI

"Herr Erlebach!" · The hunchback holds court
· "I am no longer a packhorse!" · Arrest hunchback Chulkov!
· As if a pack of dogs moulted here – · "Death to parasites!"

At that moment, Ohisver Muller lazily rose from the armchair and touched the keyboard as if playing a chord he had long ago grown tired of. Then, unperturbed, he called into the crystal calyx:

"Herr Erlebach!"

The silver circle showed Petr Brok a pale face against the black and white mosaic of tailcoats and shirtfronts. It was distorted with terror.

"Herr Erlebach!"

The face fell to the ground and the hands flew up, palms upturned.

"Mercy, mercy!" the calyx wailed.

But Ohisver Muller continued unmoved:

"Herr Erlebach! – 95! – 64! – Red mirrors, room number 7!"

A white fog then passed across the white circle and when it cleared, the silver distance had moved closer – Hotel Bar ELDORADO! – Under the opaque glass pendant lamps shaped like antediluvian skulls, the company of adventurers are sitting around an oak table. Brok read all about their business when he walked through the streets of West-Wester. – When was it? How much time had passed since then?

There were some familiar faces: the hunchback Chulkov and the armless murderer Garpona. There was also the giant who had captured Brok in a net, the defeated and humiliated General Grant, who, judging from his speech, attire and manners, had quickly adjusted to his new environment.

The hunchback is holding court:

"Well, which of you is going to catch him? Kokoko! Will you kill him with your bare feet, Garpona? Or you, Secretary, will you give him Schwartz's rose, infused with old age, to smell? Lalalala! What will you do to him, Mothleg, with your sexual tincture? – Do you know how old he is? Do you want him to be consumed with love for Princess Tamara? – Meeeh! – None of you can do anything with your gas and powders and pills! – Which of you is going to capture him? – Meeeh!"

"He's not a human being!"

"He's a god!"

"Would a god let you catch him in a net?"

"There's only one God and that's Muller!"

"The devil is stronger, then!"

"Than Muller?"

"Shhh!"

All of them put their index fingers to their lips in unison. But the hunchback continued agitating:

"You cowards! – Have you not understood what's going on? Whether he is a man or god, or nothing at all – whatever he is, he is greater, stronger and more powerful than Muller! That's why we should admit the truth, while there's still time! – And side with the one who is more powerful! Away with Muller!"

Ohisver Muller rose from his armchair again, played a few dead chords on the keyboard, and then put his lips to the crystal calyx:

"Sudar Chulkov!"

The five men jumped up around the table, chairs tumbled, glasses shattered. Their hair was standing on end, their faces blurred with terror.

Only Chulkov remained seated. His chair rattled as he pushed himself away from the table. He then grabbed his glass and threw it towards the ceiling. The faces around him followed his every movement, with an expression of astonishment, half dumb, half malicious. Petr Brok expected an explosion inside the armchair and to hear the voice whistling like a deadly bullet.

But he waited in vain... It seemed that the man in the armchair was made of stuff with no nerves and no gall. – He hummed into the microphone with an inhumanly monotonous, sleepy voice:

"Sudar Chulkov! 95! – 64! – Red mirrors, room 7!"

Brok eagerly followed the rebellious expression of the hunchback's trembling face in the miraculous circle. He saw him bang the table with his fist and shout defiantly up to the ceiling:

"I won't go – I won't go! – I've done enough for you, benefactor! Meeh! From now on, I won't lift a finger for you! I got rid of old Galio for you and how did you reward me, father? – Fifty thousand stars, of course, a divine gift! – Cock-a-doodle-doo! – Every night I watch them and crow with anger! You didn't even let me into Gedonia! You promised and you didn't keep your word! But I'll get in there, without you, you filthy bastard! You know what you can do with your fifty thousand stars? You can pay others who are foolish enough, you red-haired devil! As of today, I am no longer a packhorse – I am a human being! Lalala!"

The hunchback probably continued voicing his newly found courage towards the ceiling but Muller reached for the keyboard to silence him and cover the image of the defiant hunchback with a veil of fog.

The next to appear in the circle was a humble police inspector in uniform. Muller dictated:

"Floor 411 – West-Wester, Hotel Eldorado! – Arrest Sudar Chulkov! Imprison him in the Red Mirror Hall, 95, 64, 7!"

The police uniform melted into the fog and Muller played his keyboard again. – The glass organ now screeched and wailed, as if someone was strangling little babies. – That was what those black cats sounded like in the hotbed he had just passed. – Was there a connection between the cats on heat and this diabolical altar?

And lo and behold!

Rows of phosphorescent green eyes were staring out of the machine like a thousand cats in darkness…

The cacophony soon stopped and the circle cleared. Brok saw the camp and the slow film of the battlefield from a bird's eye view. From the barricade of the revolutionaries, it moved to the 'no man's land' between the fronts, then to the bloated ramparts of the mercenary army and into their sleeping camp.

Muller's face suddenly showed concern. The crystal throat spoke with the fiery language of grenades, wheels covered in pitch, sulphur and bombs! The large pupil now reflected the slaves' desperate attack on the barricade in detail. The wooden sides of crates and barrels were suddenly littered with blue blossoms of sulphur. Pitch caught on to splinters with burning claws. The hissing flames slurped boiling water sprayed from hoses.

And yet – it was a dead barricade! No-one loomed at the highest point of it with a banner of death! It was pathetic to see an undefended barricade being conquered with mad energy. The slaves rush forward blinded by their own frenzy. In their own fire and crackle of their bombs is the spectre of the black angel of death with a red sash – who doesn't exist!

Both Petr Brok and Muller are following the victorious conquest of the deserted barricade with the same excitement.

What a surprise!

A crowd of pitiful old men are cowering in corners with raised hands. And the conquered camp makes a pathetic picture of extinguished energy, sunken mouths, sharp chins and collapsed spines.

An army of bald heads, with ridiculously wrinkled toothless faces, crawling on their knees towards the shocked victorious conquerors. Lumps of hair underfoot, fallen from their bodies, heads and faces, as if a pack of dogs had moulted here. Even human teeth, yellow and blackened, are scattered on the ground like dragon seed.

Cheers, cries of joy and wailing pour form the loudspeaker and it is possible to tune into the noise and catch individual voices:
"It was Him! Him!"
"Petr Brok!"
"Detective!"
"God!"
"The one whose coming had been prophesied!"
"Our new god!"
"He performed a miracle!"
"He is with us!"
"Him!"
"God and detective!"
"Silence! – Silence!"
Above the falling wave of cries, a fluttering winged voice:
"Follow me!"
"The staircase is clear!"
And more cries:
"Victory!"
"Forward!"
"Death to parasites!"

XLVII

General Ox · "…trap for a trap!"
· Muller offers Brok the position of God in Mullerdom
· "My answer!" · Brok under the keyboard —

It was then that Ohisver Muller finally leapt up from his armchair. He brought both fists down on the keyboard, somewhere at the very end. His green pupils flashed and the wild symphony of cat cries pierced Brok's ears. At the same time, a new large camp appeared on the disc, with an entire army of fresh, young, merry soldiers.

Brok understood what was happening.

Ohisver Muller wanted to call up the reservists, stop the breakthrough and halt the victorious onslaught of the slaves!

The time had come for Brok to thwart Muller's intention. He had seen and heard as much as he needed to. He had seen the secret of Muller's omniscience and knew what had to be done now…

Ohisver Muller put his mouth to the calyx to issue an order to the waiting army. But Petr Brok grabbed his chin and pulled it back.

The little man seized his hand and screamed so

violently that Brok started and let him go. The red-haired dwarf commenced a mad dance around the hall and there was something so spooky, so inhumanly grotesque, in that convulsive jumping up and down that Brok began to tremble with hitherto unknown terror. He followed Muller's leaps, and when he approached the machine, Brok got his dagger ready.

"Get back!" he shouted. "Don't touch the machine! – Or you're dead!"

"Dead!" laughed Muller. – "If you kill me, you'll die with me. The whole of Mullerdom will collapse!"

Then he thrust both hands into the keyboard as if he wanted to call hell itself to the rescue!

Petr Brok let his hand holding the dagger fall, distracted by a new image in the circle. It was a film showing the army of slaves in a headlong rush down the staircase. Above the frenzied faces, drunk on easy victory blazed a red-speckled flag, like a human skin with a thousand stab wounds.

Floor after floor, a colourful avalanche of ragged rabble poured down without respite, without stopping, unimpeded. And this avalanche on the screen was accompanied by a deadly silence of the crystal loudspeaker.

Muller stares at the circle and then with a devilish curse cuts the film. – And again, the merry ringing of the reservists' camp comes back, safe and secure, somewhere far away, out of harm's way.

Muller's fingers began feverishly playing the keyboard. He screamed:

"General Ox!"

But Brok tugged at his beard so that he almost pulled it out and jerked his mouth away from the microphone in time. With the speed of lightning, he threaded one half of the double-pointed beard through the arm of the chair and tied the two ends into a naval knot.

Ohisver Muller went berserk, thrashing about like a hideous grasshopper caught by its feelers, trying to free himself form this humiliating trap. His deranged fury filled Brok with terror. He watched the dwarf-like man bite then tug at the knot and finally attempt to pull his beard out, complete with his skin.

At last he managed to bite through a strand of hair and loosen the knot. – He slowly rose – but he was surprisingly meek, like a little boy who had just received a good thrashing.

In the meantime, Brok sat down in Muller's armchair, his legs crossed, and, watching Muller out of the corner of his eye, he said:

"Well, Mr Muller – an eye for an eye, a trap for a trap! – Since you didn't keep our rendezvous at number 99, I came to see you so that I can finally have a chat!"

It was difficult to tell what Ohisver Muller's face expressed at that moment, except its own dwarfish hideousness. But his hand in a wide sleeve, resembling dry sticks in a withered bell, motioned for Brok to sit down.

"Petr Brok! – Be seated!"

"I have been sitting for a while," smiled Brok. "Do you want to tell me something?"

"Petr Brok! I acknowledge the strength and power based on your invisibility. Whether you're a man or something else, you are as invincible as I am. – Well, Petr Brok, Ohisver Muller is offering you peace and friendship. But only under certain conditions which will have to be sworn to by both sides. – We each have our secret. – My secret is Mullerdom! I know that you lost your way in it. I know about every step you made along the corridors and staircases of my kingdom. I know for sure that you are not a god. The giant caught you in a net. That's not how gods behave, gods don't run away, don't hide...

Hence, you are not a god – but I can make you into one!

Petr Brok, listen to me! I'm offering you the chance to be a deity in Mullerdom! I will make you the Lord of my world. I will be the Master and you will be the God. I will share my dominion with you. I will give you half of my treasures. And if you become a faithful God, I will be able to do even more than I have so far. – Hand in hand, we are going to continue building Mullerdom. – Higher and higher... endlessly... we will drive it up to the sky in defiance of everything and everyone!"

Muller stretched out his hand towards the armchair.

"Do you want to do this?"

Brok spat into his palm.

"This is my answer!"

Ohisver Muller wiped his hand on his green dressing gown and said with sinister calm:

"Petr Brok, be careful!

I know about you waking up on the staircase. I listened to your conversation with number 794! I know more than I've told you! If you know the secret of UNIVERSE, I know the secret of your dreams! You are no god! You are a hideous, terrible dream which you consider to be reality. Well, Petr Brok, do you still want to take on Ohisver Muller? – If you keep quiet, so will I... Look!"

Ohisver Muller showed him his left palm.

Brok felt stunned terror.

He saw the red triangle...

He quickly closed his eyes but it was too late... the triangle penetrated his brain and its sharp points pierced his temples and the back of his head –

Brok came to his senses for one last moment only to see Muller sitting in his armchair as before and hear him shout vengefully into the crystal calyx: "General Ox! General Ox!"

He closed his fist and felt the hot handle of the dagger. He realised that he had just enough strength to –!

He raised his hand and brought it down again. The steel plunged into Muller's back and into his heart.

Somewhere deep down, he could hear a thundering noise so terrible and deafening as if the moon had left its trajectory and crashed into the earth. – The four walls, floor and ceiling started to topple to one side with an incredible roar. The objects inside the room fell from the floor to the wall. The altar came crashing down on top of Brok! The iron keyboard crushed his skull.

A short sharp glassy pain came that instantly dissolved into nothing. – A colourless, shapeless nothing...

XLVIII

*The red triangle remained on the ceiling · "Be well then!"
· The dream of a thousand floors*

No-one knows how long Petr Brok's death lasted under the steel keys of Ohisver Muller's overturned organ. What happened, however, was that a nameless man who had woken up at the beginning of this story on a staircase suddenly opened his eyes and saw the ceiling, so lovely, so angelic in its bright whiteness –

And in the middle of this miraculously white ceiling there was a red triangle! The man quickly closed his eyes in terror. But, surprisingly, the triangle remained on the ceiling without hurting or jabbing him, without pressing down on him. – The man slowly glanced at it through his eyelashes, until he became certain that the triangle was painted on the ceilings and could do him no harm. On the contrary, how pleasant it was to grasp it with his eyes and reflect dreamily on his delightfully perfect, austere simplicity –

Then he heard a voice:

"Look! He's waking up…"

He turned his head.

To his surprise, he saw human faces! Real, living faces made of flesh and blood, with moving lips and blinking eyelids and brotherly smiles.

These glasses on a nose, this grey beard touched a thousand times – that must be a doctor – but there are also young, clear, smooth smiles under white caps – These are the sisters of mercy, for they have red crosses on their chests. So many beautiful faces surround the man's bed.

The doctor with the grey beard, wearing a white coat, bends over him and takes his wrist in his hand.

"You are cured!" he says. "Believe or not, it's true! – I don't believe in miracles but this is something I don't understand…"

"Where am I?" the man whispers fearfully, remembering his dream of a thousand floors.

The doctor grins:

"In the world! You should have been lying under lime in the typhoid pit behind the Totskoy camp!"

He tugged at the man's ear.

"Be well then! I myself am going to drink an extra glass to your health and will go to sleep satisfied… Do you know, you devil, that you've been raving for three days? They brought you here from the barracks of death! You've been mumbling and raving, all nonsense, arguing and jumping out of bed. In the end we had to strap you down… and all that time we couldn't wake you up. That was some kind of sleeping typhoid you had… I say, what have you been dreaming about, my son, who was that Ohisver Muller who treated you so badly?"

The House of a Thousand Floors

The patient was strangely moved, so much so he didn't listen to the grey-bearded, voluble doctor. In a split second, he remembered who he was, his past, his name, his place in the world, after he returned from captivity. – Everything had come back to him and it all made perfect sense now.

Only Ohisver Muller's name reminded him of his monstrous dream.

Half amazed, half amused, he said:

"I dreamt I was lost in a house of a thousand floors. – And Ohisver Muller – was its landlord."

Afterword

Jan Weiss is variously described as an expressionist, a surrealist, an author of fantasy, and as one of the founders of Czech science fiction, alongside Karel Čapek whose futuristic plays and novels such as *R.U.R, The Absolute at Large, Krakatit* and *War with the Newts,* are known to English-language readers. Both writers anticipated the post-war development of Czech science fiction and the work of its most prominent authors such as Josef Nesvadba and Ondřej Neff, and both had a disturbingly prophetic vision unparalleled by their successors.

Born in the town of Jilemnice in the Krkonoše Mountains in 1892, Jan Weiss went to high school in Dvůr Králové and enrolled as a law student in Vienna. He had barely completed two semesters when World War I broke out and he was drafted into the Austro-Hungarian Army in 1914 at the age of twenty-two to fight against the Allied forces. In 1916, he was taken prisoner by the Russians and spent the rest of the war in prisoner-of-war camps, notably in the infamous Totskoye camp

Afterword

in the Orenburg region in the southern Urals, a location which continued to serve as a camp for Polish prisoners in World War II and was the site of nuclear tests in the 1950s. Jaroslav Hašek, the well-known Czech author of the classic war satire *The Good Soldier Schweik*, was imprisoned in the same camp and it was there that both Weiss and Hašek contracted typhoid fever. After he was rescued and cured, Weiss joined Czechoslovak legions in Russia before returning to his homeland in 1920. He lived in Prague until his death in 1972, working as a public servant and enjoying the support of the Communist establishment which honoured him with several awards, including the Artist of Merit.

Weiss's work consists of short stories, novellas and novels. He first began writing for magazines in 1924 and the title of his very first published story was "Sen" (The Dream), presaging his preoccupation with the relationship between dream and reality characteristic of his early works. He debuted in 1927 with three collections of short stories, *Zrcadlo, které se opožďuje* (The Time Delay Mirror), *Barák smrti* (The Barracks of Death) and *Bláznivý regiment* (The Crazy Regiment).

In the short story "Barák smrti", Weiss drew on his experiences of the prisoner-of-war camp which – rather than the front – dominated the memories of his time in Russia and became one of the key sources of inspiration for his later works. The story "Bláznivý regiment" in a collection of the same name is a satire on the absurdity of war, while the eponymous story of the third collection, *Zrcadlo, které se opožďuje*, is a fantasy in which a mirror reflects whatever takes place in front of it with a time

Afterword

delay, revealing moments none of the protagonists expect to become public. He published more story collections in the following years, including *Tři sny Kristiny Bojarové* (Three Dreams of Kristina Bojarová, 1931*)*, *Nosič nábytku* (The Furniture Carrier, 1941) and *Povídky o lásce a nenávisti* (Tales of Love and Hatred, 1944), published during the war, were followed ten years later by *Příběhy staré a nové* (Tales Old and New, 1954).

Weiss began publishing predominantly sci-fi and futuristic stories in the late 1950s and early 1960s: *Země vnuků* (The Land of Our Grandchildren, 1957), *Družice a hvězdopravci* (Satellites and Astronomers, 1960) and *Hádání o budoucím* (Guessing at the Future, 1963). His short stories were very popular and continued being republished in different collections throughout the 1960s and '70s and into the 1980s.

He also published a number of novels and novellas, starting with the burlesque fantasy *Fantóm smíchu* (The Phantom of Laughter, 1927), followed by the social satire *Mlčeti zlato* (Silence is Golden, 1933) and a critique of a society deformed by capitalism *Spáč ve zvěrokruhu* (The Sleeper in the Zodiac, 1937). Then his psychological novel set in the time of German occupation of Czechoslovakia *Volání o pomoc* (A Call for Help) was published in 1946.

Dům o tisíci patrech (The House of a Thousand Floors) was Weiss's first novel. Published in 1929, it is without doubt his most accomplished and successful work, and it has continued to cast a spell over generations of readers. It was published in numerous re-editions up until the 2000s, all of which came with innovative typesetting and illustrations reflecting the style of the time.

Afterword

Weiss was known for repeatedly working with several recurring themes such as the shifting boundaries between dream and reality, both a thematic and structural element which also points to the hallucinatory states of mind induced by typhoid fever with a sense of a hyperreal yet grotesquely warped dream logic he began exploring in "Sen". The story "Horečka" (Fever), included in his first collection of short stories, is in fact the first draft of the realistic (and autobiographical) storyline of *The House of a Thousand Floors* about a soldier in a prisoner-of-war camp who, like the author, suffers from typhoid fever-induced hallucinations before being rescued and cured. Weiss then elaborated on this storyline by adding the various themes and layers which make the novel so fascinating and unusual: the fairytale theme of Petr Brok's double mission to rescue Princess Tamara, abducted by Ohisver Muller, the master of Mullerdom, the house of a thousand floors, and to engage in a battle between good and evil by seeking out and eliminating Muller himself.

The idea of Mullerdom belongs within the realms of fantasy and science fiction: the "house of a thousand floors" is both the vertical city of futuristic dreams and a dystopian empire of evil. Complete with a social hierarchy, criminal underworld, stock exchange, casinos and clubs where selected few indulge in decadent search for ultimate pleasures, it is ruled by a dictator who is worshipped as god, the seemingly omnipresent and omniscient Muller, the master of surveillance and manipulator of minds. No-one knows who Muller is or what he looks like, but he has access to everyone in Mullerdom, listening in to every conversation and watching the most intimate moments in the life of its inhabitants.

Afterword

Despite the Orwellian echoes apparent to today's reader, Mullerdom is primarily an allegory of capitalist society where ruthless exploitation and degradation of human beings fuels the spread of a revolutionary ideology, hyperbolically charting out a world where workers are fed concentrate containing the minimal nutrients required for bare survival while being deprived of everything that would make them human: spiritual life, love, desire, dignity and a purpose in life. As Brok is told by the first inhabitant of Mullerdom he meets: "We don't know what love is, and that's why our days are endless and there's no future for us except death. We have no sense of taste, we feel no hunger and we have no wishes or dreams, save for one: an amazing longing that torments us and that not even God Muller can take away from us. A longing for death!"

Space travel, a standard trope of science fiction, is another futuristic theme Weiss adopts – with a difference: like the entire house of a thousand floors, it eventually turns out to be the product of a hallucinating soldier's feverish mind, and within that dream – or nightmare – the space travel industry is shown to be a lie, a cruel trick played on the inhabitants of Mullerdom by Universe Company. Their desire to "travel to the stars" makes them victims of Muller's henchmen who strip them of their possessions, enslave them or kill them in what becomes a terrible prophecy of real horrors to come. And it is here that Weiss predicts the Holocaust with its transports, gas chambers and piles of pedantically categorised belongings, in much the same way as Čapek foresaw the use of atomic weapons in his 1922 novel *Krakatit*.

Afterword

The novel works with an array of themes favoured by Weiss's contemporaries: part dystopian fantasy, part science fiction, part fairytale with a dash of the crime genre, it is primarily a work of social criticism, less akin to pure science fiction on the one hand and to literary works exploring the Freudian theories of human psychology and the subconscious that became popular at the time on the other — like, for example, another less known Central European classic revolving around the blurred line between dream and reality, *Caliph the Stork* by Weiss's Hungarian contemporary Mihály Babits. Oscillating between hyper-real dream and nightmarish reality, the main storyline of the dream eventually gives in to the reality of a semi-conscious, dying soldier who is rescued and brought back from the dimly lit, louse-ridden camp barracks to a hospital with its soothing, clean white bed, white ceiling and white uniforms of the doctors and "sisters of mercy" who save his life, as if in an act of redemption, just as he wakes from a dream in which he had committed a murder and brought the entire house of a thousand floors crashing down.

With its humanistic message and imaginative power, *The House of a Thousand Floors* is a modern classic that still speaks to readers today as it continues to gather layers of meaning in an ever-extending framework of literary and historical references. It is a unique novel, a masterpiece of more than one genre, unusual and still fresh, that has withstood the test of time for close to a century now.

Alexandra Büchler